Carter clashed with a giant sentry.

The big man moved to crush him. Carter drew his Luger and fired three times, each shot scoring. The giant roared and grabbed him in a bone-breaking bear hug.

Carter smashed the gun against the man's head until he loosened his grip. The Killmaster wiggled free. The giant crawled to a tire iron and picked it up.

"Enough is enough!" Carter rasped.

He pumped five more slugs into the giant, and it was over.

FROM THE NICK CARTER
KILLMASTER SERIES

THE POSEIDON TARGET

KILL MASTER
NICK CARTER

JOVE BOOKS, NEW YORK

KILLMASTER #232: THE POSEIDON TARGET

A Jove Book/published by arrangement with
The Condé Nast Publications, Inc.

PRINTING HISTORY
Jove edition/December 1987

ISBN: 0-515-09324-6

Jove Books are published by The Berkley Publishing Group,
200 Madison Avenue, New York, New York 10016.
The name "JOVE" and the "J" logo
are trademarks belonging to Jove Publications, Inc.

PRINTED IN THE UNITED STATES OF AMERICA

10 9 8 7 6 5 4 3 2 1

*Dedicated to the men of the
Secret Services of the
United States of America*

ONE

The high-sided junk had barely nestled against the rickety pier when the heat haze from the land seemed to swallow the ship.

The wiry little Chinese skipper and two of his five sons swung open the port side loading hatch. This done, they all turned to face their single passenger with broad smiles.

He was tall, a few inches over six feet, and compared to the little junk captain he looked like a giant. He had wide shoulders, a rugged and scarred face, and dark hair. If one looked very close, a gray hair could be detected here and there.

"No good, North Borneo," the little skipper said. "Shitty hot, boring place with ugly women. You sure you don't want to make round trip back to Hong Kong with us?"

"No, thanks, Po," the tall passenger replied, his stern face breaking into a rare smile. "I just might find my fortune here."

"Shit, man, you crazy American. But next time you in Hong Kong, you come see me. I get you good rates at my cousin's whorehouse."

"I'll do that, Po. See you."

"Good-bye."

The little Chinese turned to his gathering family and began barking orders. As one, they turned and began bringing the cargo topside for unloading.

Nick Carter hoisted his Aussie billybag to his shoulder and dropped to the pier. Before him was the seaside port of Sandakan, on Borneo's north shore. He checked the quayside both ways, spotted a sign in the distance to his right, and headed that way.

He walked slowly. It was oppressively hot. Soon, by midafternoon, it would rain, and then by dusk the sea would cough up a little cooling breeze. But right now it was still, lifeless hot, and even flies didn't buzz in the heavy air.

A few yards from the quay, cobblestones took over from cracked concrete. Farther into the town he could see more sleepy cobbled streets winding under tapong trees. Over half the buildings still had old-fashioned thatched roofs. It was convenient. When the monsoons came and blew off the roofs, they were cheap and easy to replace.

He paused at the door under the elaborately lettered sign, SEA DOG, and gingerly rubbed his elbow along the billybag. The bulge of his favorite lady—a 9mm Luger he affectionately called Wilhelmina—was reassuring.

It's the Sea Dog, the message in Hong Kong had said. *It's right on the quay. You are Bonaparte.*

It was crazy, the whole thing was crazy, a chase halfway around the world picking up messages at every stop telling him where to go next.

Carter moved into the gloom. He paused just inside the front door to let his eyes adjust to the dimness.

The Sea Dog was like a thousand other dockside bars that ringed the South China Sea. It was a home for derelicts, drifters, out-of-work dockhands, and transient seamen. The interior was cool compared to the outside, and as Carter walked to the bar, the sour fragrance of beer assailed his nostrils.

"Would it be a pint to start the day's sweat?"

"It would," Carter replied.

The bartender, a stubby man with a belly girth wider than his shoulders, turned to the taps. He drew the beer and then made his walrus mustache do clever things as he blew off the excess foam.

"Just in?"

"I am."

"Welcome to Borneo. That'll be one dollar Malaysian or Hong Kong or American. It all evens out in the end when you're drinkin'." His speech had an Aussie-Cockney twang to it.

Carter dropped a Hong Kong twenty on the bar and lifted the pint. The beer was cold and Australian. Carter drank half the pint without lowering it. When he did, he smiled.

"Cold."

"Aye, the only bloody thing in this place that is. O'Brien, out of Brisbane."

"Bonaparte, San Francisco."

"I thought you was American," the man nodded. "Bonaparte . . . Bonaparte . . . I know the name."

"I tramped out of Manila for Hong Kong. Got drunk in Kowloon and missed my ship. A mate of mine wrote there might be something down here for me."

"Ah, I remember now. Nick Bonaparte, is it?"

"It is."

The man lifted a set of keys from his belt and moved to a large back-bar cabinet. The door swung open and Carter saw a cubbyhole divided into alphabetical slots. There was only one envelope in "B."

The Sea Dog, like so many quayside bars in the Far East, served as a private post office for transient seamen.

"There ya are. Thought I remembered the name."

Carter slipped the envelope in his pocket. "What do I owe you?"

"Just the beer. Yer mate gave me a fiver for the message."

"Then another, and let me buy you one."

"Thanks, mate." The grin grew wider.

While he drew the beers, Carter opened the envelope. It was the same small, precise handwriting he had seen on the two previous notes:

Madame Zinn's. Paradise Alley. Choose Jade. The key words are "Emerald Eyes."

"Here we are. To the ones we loved and left."

"To all of them," Carter said with a smile, and drank. "Is there a hotel nearby, not too expensive?"

"You mean cheap," O'Brien said, laughing.

"That's right. I've heard of a place called Paradise Alley."

"Ah, laddie, they don't sleep in Paradise Alley, but there's a place near there. It ain't clean, but it's cheap."

"That'll do."

"Turn left outside, go three blocks and turn left again. You'll see the Samarcan."

"Much obliged." Carter hoisted his billybag and gathered his change, leaving a dollar on the bar.

"And, laddie, if you're lookin' for a little fun in Paradise Alley tonight, watch yerself!"

"I'll do that."

He walked back into the heat, and five minutes later found the Samarcan. He checked in, took one look at the communal bathroom, and backtracked to a Chinese bathhouse he had passed.

Inside, he bathed and sat naked in a sauna with a woman fanning him while her husband laundered and pressed his white suit.

A half hour later he was back in his hotel, again naked, on the bed as the afternoon storm started. It was a solid deluge with the constant blue-white impact of lightning. By the time it had passed and moved inland, leaving the gutters in torrents and steam rising from the washed cobblestones, Carter had gone over every moment of every day in the two weeks since he had left San Francisco.

He had also gone over everything he knew about Jerome Pletov, the man who had brought him on this merry chase. . . .

At one time, Jerome Pletov had been one of the shining lights in advanced Soviet electronics. He reached the pinnacle of his craft at an early age. His Soviet fellows, as well as scientists in the West, recognized him as a true genius.

That had been eight years ago, when Pletov had contacted a high-level diplomat in the American embassy in Prague. He had taken enough under the Soviet system. Now he wanted out. He was willing to trade his brain and what it contained for freedom in the West.

The State Department, as well as Defense, was eager. Carter and a team brought him out. But once in Washington, they discovered that Pletov wasn't exactly the bargain they had been counting on.

Brilliant he was, but he was also a self-centered little egotist whose tastes ran to every excess he could find in the West that had been denied him in Russia. He wanted—and demanded—the most expensive of everything from cars to clothes to women.

And Washington indulged him.

Carter had pretty well washed his hands of the man, seeing him only occasionally when an assignment or mission could be helped by jogging Pletov's memory about a certain person or place.

For all his excesses, Pletov proved to be every bit the genius. In time, when he was cleared not to be a double or a security risk, he was given a high-level job with the huge Dollerman Electronics conglomerate.

He rose quickly in their research department, and was eventually teamed with a man named Thomas Kreskey. The two of them worked for, and with, Ansel Moultron in the top-secret marine laboratories of Dollerman in Oregon.

Then, two years earlier, all three of them had disappeared. They were on a small vessel off the coast of Oregon, along with four Navy crew members, testing underwater surveillance equipment, when the ship sank. None of the seven bodies was ever recovered.

The Pentagon, the Defense Department, and the Dollerman corporation were frantic. Evidently, Ansel Moultron and his two assistants were on the verge of a giant breakthrough in submarine warfare.

But nothing could be done; scientists, ship, and crew had gone down in water so deep that even *Glomar* couldn't find them.

At first it had been rumored that they had been pirated by a Soviet fishing vessel. But feelers both inside and outside the Soviet Union proved that the Russians had nothing to do with the disappearance.

The three scientists were written off, along with all the advances that were presumed in their heads. The project went into limbo for a while, and was eventually assigned to another team.

Then, three weeks earlier, the letter with a Bangkok

postmark came to Carter's Georgetown apartment.

Carter:

I am sure, since you detested every moment I spent with you, that you will remember me. I am also sure that you are well acquainted with the reports of my death, as well as the deaths of Ansel Moultron and Thomas Kreskey.

Well, it was a faked death. I assure you that the three of us survived the sinking ship. I can also assure you that the research we were undertaking before our so-called deaths has been completed. What was to be known as the Poseidon Device has now become a reality. I won't take the time here to go into the details, but if you want Ansel Moultron, and the device, you will follow my instructions to the letter.

You will contact only your intelligence superior. Through his inquiries, the two of you will know the importance of meeting with me and agreeing to the paltry demands I am planning to make. Whatever I could ask for is nothing in comparison to the Poseidon Device, I assure you.

If you and your superior agree, place an ad in the personals column of next Sunday's London *Times*, It should read as follows: "Josephine, I am sorry. Bonaparte."

If the ad is not in next Sunday's *Times*, I will assume you are both fools and I will turn to my old Soviet comrades. If the ad is placed, you will receive another letter at your Georgetown address, giving you specific instructions on how to reach me.

Jerome Pletov

• • •

Carter flipped his cigarette out the open window and watched it fizzle on the wet street. A stooped man with a load of wood on his shoulders looked up, cursed him with two upraised fingers for almost hitting him, and moved on.

The AXE agent moved back into the shabby room and began to dress in his clean whites.

David Hawk, head of AXE, had taken Pletov's letter seriously. Within minutes after reading it, he had put out subtle feelers.

"If what he says is true, if the three of them are alive and they have continued their research and the device works, this is dynamite."

Carter bit. "Just what the hell is the Poseidon Device?"

"It is an underwater electronics surveillance system that will revolutionize submarine warfare. For years, the Soviet Union, us, China, France, and the U.K. have been putting massive amounts of cash and brainpower into an electronics system that will make the ocean literally transparent."

Carter had listened to the rest of it with only one ear. He already knew what it meant. If a submarine could be spotted and tracked at any depth, in any weather, the spotter could take away the spottee's first-strike potential with submarine-based missiles.

It would be one hell of an advantage.

Carter was given the go-ahead. The ad was placed in the London *Times*, and the next message came:

Carter:
 So glad you have agreed. Believe me, you won't regret it. Tuesday next, the cruise ship *Pacific*

Princess sails from San Francisco. You will sail first class with the name Nick Bonaparte. You will be contacted aboard ship. It would be in both our interests if this letter and the previous one were burned.

                                        Pletov

And that's where it had begun. One night out of Honolulu, a tiny, dark and exquisite Chinese girl had slipped into Carter's cabin.

"You will fly from Honolulu to Manila. Your instructions are in this sealed envelope. This is the way you will receive your instructions from now on. If the seal on the envelope has been tampered with, you will stop where you are and place a new ad in the London *Times*: 'Josephine, I can't get home. Bonaparte.' "

"Is all this really necessary? I mean, if—"

But she was gone, and no matter how hard he tried to find her before they docked, he couldn't.

From Manila it had been as a seaman on a tramp freighter to Hong Kong, and then the junk to Borneo.

Now he had what he hoped was his last set of instructions and his last contact.

Carter took the Luger from its oilskin wrappings, checked everything for tropic rot, and slipped it into the small of his back under his belt.

A gentle breeze was wafting inland from Sandakan Harbor when he hit the streets. It was still early, so he found a café that looked cleaner than the rest, and ate.

He felt safe. What tracks Pletov hadn't covered with his elaborate precautions, Carter was fairly sure he had covered himself.

After forcing down most of the food, he hit the street again and headed for Paradise Alley.

• • •

It was, as the name implied, more alley than street. By day it was probably charming, with the sun slithering around its craggy corners. There were probably even a few kids and dogs racing each other up and down its well-worn cobbles.

What the hell, even whores have kids, especially in this part of the world, he mused.

By night it was dark and ominous. A few scattered, old-fashioned streetlights did little to cheer the place. And the fact that the evening sea breeze kept them constantly swinging on their chains didn't help.

Madame Zinn's looked more prosperous than the rest. Its masonry was rotting in only a few places, and the roof was slate instead of thatch. The main floor was a bar. Once inside, there was little doubt about the top three floors.

Besides a few bleary-eyed drinkers and a good-looking young Chinese in wide trousers and a UCLA T-shirt playing an old upright piano, there were a dozen scantily-clad girls lolling around.

Carter hit one side of the bar about the time the bartender hit the other side. His red, veined face showed years of boozing, and his big arms were a mass of purple tattooing. His paunch was cut in half by a rope holding up his pants, and he wore clogs instead of shoes.

Carter ordered beer and specified "bottle." God only knew, he thought, what might come out of the rusty tap behind the bar. It came, and Carter paid, swinging around on the stool as he sipped to survey the room.

The girls were all in their late teens or early twenties, some pretty, some not. Carter was trying to put the name Jade to one of the faces and bodies, when the kid at the piano switched from stateside honky-tonk to Chopin.

The Killmaster guessed it was a signal to Madame Zinn that a paying customer had arrived. He was right. About eight bars in, the beaded curtains at the top of the stairs parted and a short, plump woman with too much makeup on her face and a mile of blue-black hair piled on her head stepped through.

She moved down the stairs as if they were a rolling deck, spotted Carter from the bottom, and rumbled his way. The housecoat she sported for a dress had a matte finish like her face, and the ton of jewelry at her throat and jangling on her arms made her look like a '60 Buick.

"Welcome to Madame Zinn's." Her breath smelled of good scotch. "You like anything you see?"

"Maybe," Carter said and grinned.

"All Hong Kong girls, very nice, very clean."

"Depends on the price."

"You American . . . you have American money?"

"Hong Kong."

"Fifty Hong Kong dollar buy you an hour of paradise."

"Too much."

"Why you say too much—you damned cheapskate?"

"Twenty."

"No, hell no! Madame Zinn's girls best in Borneo." She was practically screaming, but no one even looked their way. "You want class fuckee, you have to pay! How much you pay?"

"Twenty-five Hong Kong."

"Fucking cheapskate. Which girl you like?"

"I like names," Carter said. "Carmen, Lucinda, Jade . . ."

"I have all those." She pointed a stubby finger and three girls cruised over.

"What's your name?" Carter asked.

"Luang . . ."

"She Carmen," Madame Zinn said, glaring.

Carter checked the eyes of all three: they would be the key for Pletov. The gaze of two of them was dull and listless. The girls were probably on hash, or something stronger. The youngest of the three was a better bet. Her brown eyes were modestly lowered, but Carter could see brightness and alert intelligence in them.

Pletov would insist on that. An idiot or someone whose brain was wasted with dope or booze couldn't be hypnotized.

"What's your name?"

"Jade."

"How you know that, sailor?" Madame Zinn cackled.

"Sixth sense."

Carter paid and followed the girl upstairs.

The room was half dark and the bed was unmade. Cards, bottles, glasses, and clothing were scattered all over the floor. And the floor itself was grimy, as if someone had given up cleaning it.

"I give you good time, you give me tip." She had a smooth voice, low in pitch, and she spoke in English in the manner of one who had learned from an Englishman.

Carter turned. She had been wearing an emerald green *sumong* dress, high on the neck and slit to her hips on the sides. Now the dress was on the floor and she was naked.

She was a small girl with tawny brown skin, and when she moved she displayed the sinuous grace of a cat. Her waist was slim, her hips just full enough, and her breasts high.

"Sure, a big tip," Carter said, slipping out of his jacket and sitting down to take off his shoes.

They chatted about nothing as Carter went through the motions of undressing. Then he hit her with it.

"They say that for a woman to deserve the name Jade, she should have emerald eyes."

Carter had seen it happen many times to many people, but never quite as complete nor as fast.

The girl stiffened where she sat on the bed. She blinked twice and then those dark, wide-set eyes grew detached and glassy. He moved into a crouch directly in front of her.

"Can you hear me?"

"Yes, of course."

"I am Bonaparte," he said.

"Hello, Mr. Bonaparte. What do you want of me?"

"Have you a message for me from Mr. Phipps?"

"Yes. You are to go to Turtle Island. When you arrive, you will check into the Lampali resort. You will be contacted by Djumi. Do you understand?"

Carter did. It was a neat twist. Turtle Island was about twenty-five miles north of Sandakan, in the Sulu Sea. Lampali was a health resort for rich nuts who wanted to sweat off a couple of pounds in a mini-paradise because they didn't have anything else to do.

Whatever kind of escape Pletov was making, and from whom, he had planned it well.

"Is that all you were to tell me?"

"Yes."

Slowly, Carter went through the mumbo jumbo of erasing everything from her memory, and then awakened her.

"How come you no undress?"

"I've changed my mind. It's an old wound and very embarrassing." He pressed a twenty, Hong Kong, in her hand. "You won't tell anyone, will you?"

She shrugged. "No difference to me."

Carter slipped his jacket on and went downstairs. Madame Zinn cackled at him from the bar.

"What I tell you? Good, huh?"

"I'll never be the same again," Carter replied, and hit the street.

TWO

There was helicopter service to Turtle Island, but Carter disdained it. Instead, he caught the morning boat that delivered supplies.

Before leaving, he dumped the billybag in favor of a decent suitcase, and bought two changes of leisure clothing. Checking into a resort like Lampali also called for a fresh shave and haircut.

The trip took three hours under crystal-clear, cloudless skies. Carter walked the short distance to the sprawling Lampali compound and checked in as James Barron, a travel writer. Rather than a cabana, he chose a small suite in the main hotel building.

Settled in his room, he telephoned David Hawk on the AXE chief's private line with an update.

The reception was a little sour, but Carter had expected it. With trouble spots erupting all over the world, a merry chase around the South China Sea was the last assignment he wanted to give his top agent.

"I did a little more digging, N3. At the rate research is going, a lot of experts have predicted that it will be a good ten years before technological solutions are found and Moultron's brainchild becomes a truly operational system."

Hawk's words told Carter the tale. If Moultron was alive, and if the system had been perfected *now*, everyone would be after him and it.

"That means, whatever Pletov wants, he gets?" The words left a bad taste in Carter's mouth.

"It looks that way. But stall and dicker as much as you can."

"I'll do that for sure."

Carter hung up and took a long, cold shower. Then he slipped into a pair of trunks and hit the pool. Ten laps and he fell on a chaise to bake some of his frustration out in the sun.

"Something to drink, sir?" It was a bare-chested waiter dressed like a Polynesian beachboy.

"Yeah, something cool with gin."

"Yes, sir."

Two minutes later he was back with a tray, setting up the table by Carter's chaise. The Killmaster was two sips into the drink when he spotted a tent card on the tray. It was touting the evening's entertainment in the Lampali's lounge, the China Sea.

The strikingly beautiful face staring out at him from the center of the card belonged to the girl who had given him the instructions on the *Pacific Princess*.

Above the picture was a name: Anna Djumi.

The China Sea was a glittering, American-type lounge. Carter deliberately came early and got a tiny triangular table half hidden in a red-padded niche along one wall. He ordered brandy and sipped it slowly as the place began to fill up.

When the room was about a third full—mostly Chinese, a few Australians, some Brits from Hong Kong, and two sets of overweight American newlyweds—a dark young man appeared on the stage. He proceeded to try to sing, and did vicious things to an undeserving piano.

The evening wore on. Carter ordered a second and then a third brandy as the babble of conversation around him grew. Eventually he could no longer hear the words of the singer, and a blue layer of cigarette smoke hung beneath the low ceiling.

At ten sharp the piano player disappeared and a guitarist came on. He was dressed from the hips down in a brilliant red batik cloth. His smooth brown skin shone with oil and resembled copper. He played with assurance—and some skill—for a few minutes, and then a girl moved from among the backstage draperies into the shifting colors of a spotlight.

Even expecting her, it was still a bit of a shock. It was the girl from the *Pacific Princess*, all right. But what a difference.

She had the poise and the sleek strength of a leopard. She wore a costume of sheer silk, a combination kemban and sarong, the kemban a tight twist of silk around her breasts, the sarong flowing light as gossamer to the floor, floating as she moved, wrapping around her naked feet as she spun slowly to the rhythm of the guitar. The material was brown like her body, and with the spotlight also in hues of tan, pink-amber, and brown, the material seemed not to exist, to be only a mist of changing intensity through which her body was visible, uncertain, drifting, like viewing a naked swimmer through a brownish-greenish sea.

She started slowly, with movements of her feet and shoulders. She was extremely graceful. She seemed to dance for her own amusement, unconscious of the eyes that followed her. She danced with her head up, smiling, but scornful of applause or favor or anything that the club's patrons could confer.

Then, with a change of tempo, the guitarist began to sing. He paused, and without stopping her dance, she responded. She didn't have a good singing voice, it was almost a monotone, but there was something compelling about it. Her voice was steady and it did something. It stirred, arousing some half-remembered urge, like moonlight and warm winds, like regrets and a half-forgotten love.

A peculiar spell was woven by guitar and voices and the veiled naked beauty of the dancer. But the mood kept changing. The time for singing was over. She danced rapidly, leading rather than following the guitar, until suddenly, with a toss of her head, a swing of her long hair, a wild sway of her supple body, it was over. She spun to leave, and for the first time actually looked at her audience. And her eyes came to rest on Carter.

He returned her stare and, for a brief instant, she seemed to be smiling.

Then she was gone.

The lights came up and the babble started again.

Fifteen minutes later she appeared in a figure-fitting white dress that emphasized her full breasts and gleamed against her skin. She moved through the tables, exchanging greetings, signing autographs, and accepting praise for her act. Now and then she would linger, sitting at a table and chatting. Once she even accepted a drink, so it took practically a half hour before she reached Carter's table.

"Good evening."

"Good evening. Could I buy you a drink?"

Once she was in the booth and fresh drinks were brought, she leaned forward and lowered her voice.

"And so we meet again, Mr. Bonaparte."

"Where is he? I'm tired of the chase."

"It has been long, I agree." She slid around the booth until their thighs were touching and one full breast was pressed against his arm. "Now you must seduce me . . .

with your eyes, your lips, your smile, until I can no longer stand it.''

"Look, lady, I love fun, but this is business . . .''

"Yes, it is,'' she said, showing perfect white teeth. "That is why it must appear that you excite me so much that I let you accompany me back to my bungalow.''

For the next half hour Carter seduced. Finally she was satisfied and they left, arm in arm, laughing.

It was a short walk across the pool area and down a narrow walk between leafy trees.

"This one,'' she said, pulling a key from her purse.

When the door was open and the light was on, she turned and moved into his arms. Her pouting red mouth seemed to glide upward and her lips found his. Her arms came around his neck and, as the kiss deepened, she clung to him tighter and her body started moving.

"Is this necessary?''

"Yes,'' she murmured, "in case someone is watching.''

Finally she broke the clinch and came up for air. Without another word, she pulled him inside and kicked the door closed.

"The bedroom is in here.''

Carter followed her. In the bedroom, she snapped on the light and began removing her dress.

"Those venetian blinds are partially open,'' Carter noted.

"That's the idea. Take your clothes off.''

"Who the hell is watching us?'' he said, stripping and feeling like an idiot.

"No one, I hope.''

"Just what is in this for you, Anna Djumi?''

"Money, among other things. I get instructions, I follow them . . . for enough money . . . and other things.''

She dropped the last of her underthings and stretched languorously like a cat before moving across the room toward Carter.

As he followed her with his eyes, he wondered just how far this was going to go.

She had attractive legs, on the slim side but lithe and vital. Her eyes were dark. She wore her long hair wound around the crown of her head in a chic and sexy style. She was slim except in the chest, where her breasts were almost as round as cantaloupes, soft but with plenty of firmness underneath. Prominent beige-colored aureoles spread over their upper slopes and crests, the nipples at their centers strikingly erect.

She did another number with her lips and body, and then moved past him.

"Get in bed."

He did. The light went off. He heard the pad of her feet and then she was beside him, soft and warm. He was about to ask, when she answered.

"If anyone has picked up your trail, they will be watching us now."

"That would figure . . . yeah," Carter sighed, keeping his hands balled into fists.

"You can go out the kitchen window in the rear. Just below the window there are rocks and then the water. There is no place for anyone to hide back there to see you leave."

"You're sure all this is really necessary?"

He felt her shrug. "According to him, it is."

"Look, why don't you go tell that bastard—"

Her finger touched his lips. "I only do and say what I am told. I don't ask questions. I can't afford to. Believe me, the man you have come to see has given me what I most desire. I ask no questions beyond what is promised."

"Which is?"

"In time you may learn that. When you leave, stay among the rocks until you get around the lagoon. Once there, you will see the compound of the cabanas. Mr. Phipps is in twenty-four. It is green with white shutters. Go in the rear door. It will be unlocked."

"When?"

"Now. Get dressed in the dark. He is waiting for you."

Carter slid from the bed and dressed in the darkness.

"If I don't see you again, Anna Djumi, it's been swell."

"Oh, you'll see me again, Mr. Bonaparte."

As Carter crawled out the kitchen window, he tried to figure out the odd tone in her voice.

Over the rocks was no easy trip, but he finally made it and vaulted the low wall into the compound. In front of him was a wide wooden promenade leading down the rear of the dimly lit or dark cabanas.

As he moved, he checked the numbers. Most were dark, but number 21 had a lantern on the outer deck. It threw a discreet and revealing light on a ravishing blonde who lay back on a chaise longue, dreaming upward in the moonlight. She wore a very brief bikini, and seemed about to burst out of its tiny triangles.

She looked up as Carter started past. "Oh, hello there." The accent was British.

"Hello. I'm just out for a little air."

"Beautiful night for a swim."

"Yes . . . yes, it is."

He rushed on toward the last cabana in the line. It was number 24.

There was no sound now but the soft lapping of the sea against the rocks. There were no lights in 24, leaving the lounges and canvas deck chairs blue in the moonlight of the outer deck.

Carter moved forward, filling his hand with the Luger and being careful to avoid the furniture.

He slid one of the doors, trying to do it very gently and cursing the noise it made gliding along the track. When it was open far enough, he slipped his body through and dropped to the floor.

Then he saw him, about twenty feet ahead dead center in the room, lying facedown.

Damn! Carter thought, crawling ahead, the Luger out in front of him. *Halfway around the world and the bastard is dead!*

The man was very still. He wore a white jacket and dark trousers. A kris dagger, its foot-long, wavy blade shining dully in the moonlight, lay between his outstretched arms. Slowly, Carter rolled him over. The face was Chinese, young and smooth.

"Carter?" The voice sounded calm and polite.

The Killmaster rolled out of the moonlight as far as he could, the Luger up and ready.

"It's me, Carter, Pletov. You can put the gun away. I don't think they'll send anyone else tonight."

"Who is he?"

"Beyond being a Chinese, I really don't know. But since he tried to kill me, I rather imagine he worked for Dr. Chan Lee Sung."

"Look, Pletov—"

"No, *you* look, Carter. I can see you and you can't see me. I have a silenced magnum pointed at the top of your head. Now, you crawl across the hall and into the bathroom."

Carter had no choice. He slid the Luger into his belt and began to crawl.

THREE

It was a scene directly out of some grade-B adventure flick, thought Carter. He had run, like a puppet, halfway around the world, with Jerome Pletov pulling his strings.

Now the two of them sat on the floor of a windowless bathroom with towels filling the crack at the bottom of the door to shield any light from escaping. And in the adjoining room a Chinese assassin lay dead. To top it off, Pletov was calmly uncorking a bottle of Russian vodka.

"All right, Pletov, just what the hell is this all about?"

"You're sure you won't have some? It's the very best."

Carter accepted one of the glasses, to stem his anger at the other man's coolness if nothing else. The Russian filled his own glass and raised it in a toast.

"To capitalism!"

He drank and tapped the excess moisture from his pencil-thin mustache with a hand towel. Carter's earlier dislike flooded back over him like a fog.

Pletov was big, thick but not fat. Right now his shirt was unbuttoned to his belt, revealing a chest and abdomen slabbed with thick muscle. His skin was perfectly hairless and rather pink. He was medium complexioned, his hair was dry blond, and his eyes were a very bright blue. His face, while broad, was not Slavic in the manner of so many big men of his race. Were it not for a morose expression, he would have been fairly good-looking. He had a good jaw and nose, and he had breadth across his cheekbones that took the roundness from his face. He was about forty.

Pletov finished the glass and leveled his gaze on Carter. "To the business at hand. How much were you and your mysterious superior able to learn about the project?"

Carter told him the details, plus the ten-year supposition—that it would take that long to have a reliable, working device.

Pletov smiled wryly. "Wrong, I assure you. We had the basic tenets of the system worked out six months before we disappeared. Since that time it has been perfected and tested. It works."

"Okay," Carter replied, "so much for the system. Now, why the disappearance?"

"Simple . . . greed. The three of us are brilliant, but we were still no more than hired hands for Dollerman and the government. Once the system was proven, it would have been taken from us and we would have been shunted off to perfect another project, and again for peanuts."

"That's not the way I heard it," Carter retorted. "Moultron was making nearly a million a year, you and Kreskey about half a million each."

"As I said, peanuts. When we were sure we had the key, Ansel approached Kreskey and myself with a proposition. We fake our deaths, go into hiding with our own personal laboratory, and finish the device for ourselves."

"And then?"

"And then we put it out for the highest bid, with the

floor bid starting at one hundred million. I'm sure even you can see that the final price would come to far more than our yearly salaries.''

Carter had to clench his hands in hip lap to keep from reaching out and very quietly strangling Pletov.

"How come you're on the run?"

"Because Ansel is a greedy egomaniac. We named the device after Poseidon, the greek god of the sea, but in his eyes, *he* is the god. When our little plan came down to the wire, he planned on killing Kreskey and me and taking the whole for himself. I suspected as much and warned Kreskey. Thomas was a fool. Now he's dead.''

"And Moultron has someone after you."

"Several someones, I'm afraid. I thought I covered my tracks well, but Dr. Sung has eyes all over this part of the world. Evidently I was spotted somewhere along the way."

Carter knew of Dr. Chan Lee Sung. He was the top crime lord in Southeast Asia, and had contacts reaching to every corner of the globe. The base of his power was raw opium, but his tentacles stretched into everything from petty prostitution to murder for hire.

"How did Sung get involved?"

"Ansel brought him into it for two reasons: we needed bankrolling for the laboratory and equipment, and we needed protection.''

Carter sighed and reached for the bottle. "So your slimy little deal went sour. Why contact us?"

"Several reasons, revenge being not the least of them. I want now the same thing I wanted when all this started . . . enough money to live the rest of my life in comfort.''

"And how much comfort do you need?"

"I figure fifteen million will do it." Carter started to blow, but Pletov held up his hand, palm out, to stop him. "I am sure your superiors will see the wisdom in spending fifteen instead of one hundred."

Carter drained his glass and felt the harsh liquid burn its way into his gut. "Okay, what do we get for fifteen?"

"As I'm sure you know, Dr. Sung's base of operations is Hong Kong. The original laboratory was set up on one of the outer islands. Since then, it has been moved to a testing and demonstration site."

"Where?"

"I don't know—yet. But I will know in a few days' time. Then someone will lead you to that site."

"No good," Carter growled. "Too chancy."

"I have one other thing to sweeten the pot."

"Such as?"

"The finished plans to the device."

"You have them?"

"I do, and so does Ansel."

"You sneaky bastard," Carter rasped, unable to keep a flush from creeping into his face. "You want me to get rid of Moultron."

Pletov smiled. "Precisely. Once you do that, you will hopefully get his set. Of course they will do you little good without mine as well. If you have the device and I sell it to the Soviets, then it's a stalemate. And we both know, Carter, that stalemate isn't acceptable in this business. Only winning, getting the upper hand in offense and defense, is acceptable."

Carter hated to admit it, but he knew Pletov was right. He would have to go after Ansel Moultron and get his copy of the plans before the bidding took place. Then he would have to deal with Pletov for the second set.

"I can tell by the look on your face that you agree," the Russian said smugly.

"I don't have any choice."

"Precisely."

"What are the terms?"

Pletov handed him a slip of paper. "That is the number of my account at the Eurobank in Zürich. Deposit half the money. As soon as I have confirmed that it is done, I will inform Anna Djumi of the location."

Carter didn't try to mask his surprise. "What's her stake in this?"

Pletov's smile was enigmatic. "Precisely the same as mine . . . greed and revenge. I presume you have read the complete file on Ansel Moultron?"

"I have."

"Well, Carter, it is not quite complete. Years ago, Moultron had a mistress. She was half black and half Chinese. Times have changed now, of course, but in those days such a mistress was extremely unacceptable for a man of Moultron's stature. The mistress got pregnant and insisted that Moultron marry her. At the time, he was passing her off as his maid. Of course, marrying his maid—especially one who was half black and half Chinese—would be career suicide. Are you following me?"

"Go on."

"Moultron tried to have her killed. That was his first business deal with Dr. Sung. But the two assassins botched the job. The woman fled and she had her child, a daughter. Moultron kept the dogs after her for years. Finally they found her in Singapore."

"They killed her."

"Horribly, I'm afraid, right in front of the daughter. However, they made the silly mistake of letting the little girl live. She grew up in abject poverty, with one thought giving her reason for survival. Revenge."

Suddenly it all fit. "Anna Djumi."

"Bravo, Carter. You do have a logical mind." He stood. "I suggest we change clothes now. We're about the same size, so it shouldn't be a problem."

"Change clothes?"

"Yes. You see, Dr. Sung never sends just one assassin: they always work in pairs. By now I imagine that the second one—who was probably watching Anna's bungalow—has gotten curious about his comrade."

Carter could hardly believe the man's gall. "You want me to walk out of here in your clothes and lead him away?"

"Bravo, again! After all, it's only fair. I've done in one of them. You can do your part with the other one!"

"And what if he gets me? Your little plan goes up in smoke."

"Oh, I hardly think that's possible. I've seen you at work, remember? You're quite good at what you do."

Carter started to undress. "When this is over, Pletov . . ."

"Don't even think of it. I've been planning my final disappearance for too long. Not even you will be able to find me."

As Carter dressed in the other man's clothes, he had no idea of how meaningful Pletov's words would become.

Carter looked back once, just before he slid the door closed. Pletov was crouched by the front door of the cabana, waiting to make his escape once Carter drew off the hounds . . . if hounds there were.

He was big, bigger and heavier than Carter, but he moved like lightning. He came at the Killmaster in a crouch, from the small rear deck of the bungalow two up from Pletov's.

Carter saw his bulk first, and then moonlight glinting

off the blade of a knife coming straight up toward his gut.

Carter had no time to go for the Luger. He threw himself to the side and grabbed for the other man's knife hand. He managed to find the knuckles and change the blade's direction as the other man's momentum carried them both to the ground.

Carter ended up on top, pushing the knife into the grass while the hulk beneath him kicked and struggled, grabbing at Carter's hair with his free hand.

The Killmaster could see his face now in the bright moonlight. This one was Chinese, too, but much bigger than the one Pletov had shot.

As the Chinese pulled at Carter's hair, trying to drag his head back and snap his neck, he also brought a knee up hard against the Killmaster's hip. The blow sent Carter rolling to the side with his assailant right after him.

The knife came up for a thrust, but Carter managed to get a grip on the moving wrist. He knew that, if the knife hand got free again, chances were good that the Chinese had the speed and experience to kill him easily.

Both men were on their sides now, with the Chinese using his strength and agility to carry his body through with the roll so that he gained the advantage of having Carter beneath him.

Suddenly the Chinese let go of Carter's hair. Now he had both hands on the knife, his chest against the hilt, forcing the blade down. The sharp tip reached Carter's cheek, pressing the skin inward until the flesh broke. The Killmaster could feel warm blood trickling down across his throat.

Until now, the struggle had been silent. Suddenly the Chinese began to grunt with the effort of applying more and more pressure.

Carter had both his hands around the shaking wrist. He tried to push the straining blade away, but he felt it slowly sinking into his cheek. The man's strength was amazing. In seconds, Carter knew the blade would burst through into the cavern of his mouth and on into his throat.

Then the Chinese roared and raised his body for a final lunge, a gleam of triumph in his wide, flat face.

That was a mistake.

Carter heaved upward at the same time. The Chinese resisted, but he was too late. The Killmaster managed to roll, avoiding the blade. He felt it slice his ear and go by to plunge into the ground.

Before his opponent could react, Carter banged both the man's ears with the heels of his hands. The Chinese cried out in agony and rolled free.

Carter came up on one knee, pulling Wilhelmina out at the same time. But he barely managed to flick the safety off before the Chinese rolled backward and kicked. The sharp toe caught Carter's forearm, and the Luger clattered across the cement deck of the cabana.

The Chinese was on his feet in a crouch, the knife darting back and forth between his two hands. They circled, Carter watching the man's eyes instead of the knife. He could gauge the man's attack better by following the movement of his eyes.

The eyes widened slightly before he lunged. It was enough to give Carter warning. He threw himself to one side, ducking low. The blade caught his shirt and sliced some skin, but not enough to do more than draw blood.

But he had an opening. He whirled, stepped forward, and brought his knee flush up into the man's face. Bone crunched, blood squirted, and the Chinese came upright with an animal howl.

Carter glued his fingers together and rammed them

swiftly up into the man's neck.

Never look in the eye. Cardinal rule. Keep your eyes on the spot, on the throat, lock on it, and let fly.

Carter did, with all he had.

His hand whipped into flesh, propelled not only by the momentum of his swinging arm, but also by the entire weight of his body.

His timing was perfect.

His full force was concentrated in the muscles of his right shoulder and arm at the instant of impact.

Carter left his feet when he connected. He hit the man so hard that the windpipe was crushed and the left jugular vein collapsed in its own vacuum.

The Chinese fell like a rock, and Carter staggered across a nearby table, dragging it to the floor with him.

He was trying to focus his eyes and struggle to his feet, when he saw her. It was the ravishing blonde, only now she wasn't in the bikini. She wore a heavy sweat shirt, slacks, and jogging shoes.

A flash went off, momentarily blinding him.

"What the hell . . ."

By the time his eyes readjusted, she was gone. He could hear the sharp slaps of her shoes running down the boardwalk.

It took him a full minute before he found Wilhelmina and could give chase.

By the length of two cabanas he gave up. He knew it was useless. The roar of a powerful launch told him so.

He turned and backtracked to Anna Djami's bungalow.

"Good God, what happened?"

"Lots," he rasped, staggering past her into the living room. He lurched to a sideboard and a bottle of scotch. She came to his side, tightening a belt around the robe she had pulled on.

"Are you going to die?"

"Do you give a damn?"

"More than you think," she said, her eyes hard. "Tell me."

"Tell you what?"

"Did the two of you come to an agreement?"

"If we did, do you have instructions?"

"Yes. We are to go to Hong Kong and stay out of sight until he contacts us."

"Then pack while I go back to my room to clean up and change. Can you get a boat to take us back to the mainland?"

"Tonight?"

"You bet your ass tonight, honey. There are a couple of dead people over there, and I don't want to stick around and answer questions about how they got that way."

"I'll be in your room in fifteen minutes."

Carter grabbed the bottle and staggered out the door.

FOUR

For several extra dollars, the boatman took them around the headland and directly into Kota Kinabalu. As it was, it was nearly dawn by the time they landed, and pushing eight by the time an ancient taxi dropped them at the small airport.

They were lucky: there was one flight a day to Hong Kong direct. They just made it, after a quick breakfast of fruit and coffee. All through the twenty-minute wait in the boarding area, there was a tense silence between them. Every few seconds each of them would look around, expecting to see the muzzle of a gun pointing their way.

At last the flight was called. They went through customs and passport control, and took their seats. There were fifteen other passengers. Carter counted them and took stock: a few British, an American couple, and a group of Chinese. The Chinese looked like a family, complete with kiddies.

The takeoff was smooth, and by the time they reached cruising altitude, Carter was already burrowing down in his seat.

"What are you doing?"

"Sleeping," he yawned.

"You can sleep?"

"Like a baby."

And he did, until she poked him awake. "'The seat

33

belt light is on. We're landing.''

"Good.'' He stretched and buckled up. Then he came completely awake and noticed that she was staring at him. "Something wrong?''

"I've been wondering for the last hour . . . how did you get your gun through the metal detector at the airport?''

"I didn't. Remember when I left you for a few minutes in the coffee shop?''

"Yes.''

"I broke it down and air-mailed it to myself in Hong Kong at the Hotel Lilium.''

She grinned. "I think I'm going to enjoy hunting with you.''

They banked, and Carter could see the white roofs of Kowloon crawling up from the harbor. Then another bank and they were coming in low from the north. One last lazy swoop and they settled down at Kai Tak Airport. Carter got their bags from beneath the seats.

"Keep your eyes open going through customs.''

"I will. Where is this Hotel Lilium?''

"On the Hong Kong side. The owner is an old friend, very discreet. We'll take the ferry over.''

Customs was quick, not much more than a cursory glance. Carter took her elbow and used his shoulder to get through the milling crowd.

"Spot anybody familiar?''

"No,'' she replied.

"I did.''

"Who?'' she whispered, alarm in her voice.

"A local M16 man. He knows me and spotted me. I'll have to tell them why I'm here. It's protocol.''

"Must you?''

"Sure, we're on vacation.''

She just shook her head as he guided them into the

taxi line. When it came their turn, Carter quickly moved aside. A Chinese couple took the cab meant for them, and he led Anna to the next one in line.

"You are cautious."

"That's why I'm alive. The ferry," he instructed the driver.

The car flew along a cypress-lined avenue. White villas sprawled under red roofs. They passed a polo field, a group of players hacking around it.

"I understand you've been to Hong Kong before," Carter said, looking out the window.

"I grew up in Hong Kong, after Singapore. Do you know, in all those years I was never on this, the Kowloon, side?"

"That's because only the affluent live on the Kowloon side." Now he rolled his head around to look at her.

"That's right," she said softly. "How much did he tell you?"

"Not enough," Carter replied. "But I'm a patient man. You'll tell me when you're ready."

They were silent on the ferry and in the cab, right up until they pulled up in front of the Lilium.

"This is Po Chong, the red-light district!" Anna cried.

"That's right," Carter answered brightly, "but the Lilium is legit. You'll see."

Inside, the hotel was like a church—tiled, cool, quiet. Beyond the desks, an arch led to a patio hung with brilliant creepers. Tables and chairs were set around a fountain that played into a basin.

At one of the tables sat the Fat Man. His real name was Morris Purdue, but few people knew it and he never used it. Just a mention of the Fat Man anywhere in Southeast Asia and everyone knew who he was.

He looked up over his paper as Carter and Anna entered. At once a wide smile split his features. He rose, inflated his great stomach, and joined them.

"Nicholas, my friend," he said in a low monotone, "it has been far too long."

The handshake was warm and Carter returned it. "And this is my friend."

"Of course. Mademoiselle is very beautiful." He kissed Anna's hand and turned back to Carter. "Queenie is in her apartments. She will want to see you."

"Later," Carter replied. "We need two rooms connecting, and no names on the register."

"Ahh," said the Fat Man, gingerly reaching up and touching the bandage on Carter's cheek, "the visit is not exactly a holiday."

"Not exactly."

"One moment."

He waddled away, and Carter turned to Anna. "Did you sleep at all on the plane?"

"No."

"Then you're probably beat. Go on up. I want to talk to the Fat Man for a moment."

The big man returned with two keys and a young Chinese boy. "Charley has no ears and very weak sight. He will scour Hong Kong for anything you need during your stay."

The boy took both bags and trotted away with Anna trailing behind.

"I never forget a face, particularly a beautiful one," the Fat Man murmured. "I've seen that one before."

"Anna Djumi. Supposedly, she grew up in Hong Kong. I want everything you can get on her."

"You will have everything down to the size of her underwear by this evening," the Fat Man replied, watching the woman step into the elevator.

"Also, if she leaves, I want to know where she goes, if she sees anybody. If she sends a wire, I want to know what it says, and if she uses the phone, I want a tape of it."

The Fat Man laughed and his whole body laughed with him. "As usual, it will take the whole staff to accommodate your wishes. But, of course, it will be done."

Carter smiled. "You know where to send the bill."

"Of course."

"I'll also need a car and driver. It would help if he were armed."

"It will be waiting in the alley by the kitchen entrance in fifteen minutes."

"I won't need it until this evening. I think it might be better to move around after dark."

"As you wish."

"And tell Queenie I would love to join her for a late dinner."

"It will be done."

Again the two men shook hands, and Carter headed for the elevator.

"This is fine, boy, right here."

The ricksha boy stopped, lowered the front, and the man stepped down. He was a robust man with stormy gray hair that tossed about over a deeply lined, scholarly brow. He wore a nondescript raincoat, and his six-foot-plus frame must have appeared a full nine feet to the young boy who stood just above his belt buckle.

A pair of shaggy dark brows might have appeared sinister to the boy were it not for the left one, which was in constant, nervous motion. It seemed to rise and fall with the timbre of his voice. But the eyes were the man's

most fascinating feature. They were dark and mysterious, darting everywhere.

He paid off the ricksha boy and stood with an umbrella rolled under one arm, listening while the wheels
faded away across the broken pavement. It was quiet
then, with none of the nearby wharves in operation. The
area was poorly lighted. Only a few of the warehouses
that stood in solid ranks back from the harbor had been
painted or repaired during recent years, and what poor
light came from the high post lights was quickly absorbed
by the prevailing rust and gray dilapidation. Here and
there a passageway ran back among the buildings, each
of them deep canyons of blackness.

Well, blackness suited his purpose. He hefted the umbrella and walked, openly, taking his own good time,
his manner one of a person about a habitual piece of
business, as if accustomed to coming down there to the
wharves at that hour.

Actually, the area was not deserted at all, merely
quiet, sleeping: a driver was asleep in his truck; on the
junks and tramps and sailing praus that used the docks,
crews were asleep on deck; coolies were asleep on grass
mats against the buildings. He walked quietly, as if fearing to disturb them.

He passed from paving to planks that sounded hollow
beneath his feet. He could hear the ringing sound of
water slapping against pilings below.

Everything had a stamp of age. Night coolness
sharpened the odors, giving the sea a vinegary fragrance. His nerves were taut, and as often happened
to him, he had a sensation of being watched, but it
wasn't strong. It was more as if the sleeping coolies
would open their eyes on him after he had gone by.

From somewhere came the muffled dissonant twang-
ing of Chinese instruments. He passed a low, dark, di-

lapidated building. Its door was open and he caught the acrid warmth of opium. No light, no sound, but the smokers were there, somewhere, down some zigzag passageway, stretched out on unyielding shelves of boards having their "one-pipe-a-dolla."

He continued walking, moving beneath the black shadow of some metal awnings. The next building was the Eurasian warehouse. He stopped and watched.

It was a large, low building of several gables, one section added to the others. It had fallen into a state of disrepair like everything else in the area, blended by time into a single, grayish unit. A couple of covered wharves had been built out into the bay. Only the closer of the two showed signs of recent use. A small motorboat was tied there, a single light in her forecastle, but no one in sight, not even the customary native asleep by her landing stage. Everything was right, everything was as it should be. He did not even have that feeling of a trap about to be sprung.

Still he waited a while. An old man, a coolie, came past talking to himself, passing so close to him in the shadow that he could have reached out and touched him. Then he was gone, taken in by the night.

He went on, straight past the warehouse office, only glancing in as a man ordinarily would. There was a dim light on. He had a glimpse through unwashed, barred windows of a brownish, cluttered interior, a desk, some filing cabinets. He kept walking. He passed between the wharves and the warehouse. There a plank walk turned and led back between the warehouse and that of another concern next to it. It was so dark there, beneath the projecting pagodalike eaves, that he had to grope ahead of him for the handrail, and each change of level, each broken plank, gave him the uncomfortable sensation of stepping into a void.

He found a short ramp, climbed it, and the walk was terminated by a squarish landing large enough for hand trucks to maneuver.

And then, out of the darkness, two young Chinese silently emerged. They looked even more incongruous to the area than he did, dressed as they were in neatly tailored suits, white shirts, silk ties, and Burberry coats.

Two pair of black eyes scrutinized him; one nodded, and they both disappeared back into the darkness.

He entered the warehouse. It stretched out deep and far in two directions, a black-shadowed infinity filled with the straight forest of pillars that supported the roof. The pillars reflected light, rendering his eyes unable to explore the deeper limits of the building. Opposite him was the central partition of the warehouse, what once had been an outer wall, for the remnants of some Chinese advertising signs still remained. The room contained only some lumber, long webbed over and dusty; and a heap of rat-chewed sago baskets.

Rickety wooden steps climbed the far wall to a walkway. He moved toward them as an odor filled his nostrils. It was a musky odor, the kind one smells in an old barn. He knew of only one thing in the world with such a smell. Raw opium.

It brought a smile to his face. Only in the warehouses of Dr. Chan Lee Sung would the odor be so flaunted.

He climbed the stairs to the walkway where another well-dressed guard opened a door for him. Through the door was another world, a world of thick Oriental carpets, European and Asian antique furniture, walls heavy with art, and Dr. Chan Lee Sung.

He sat, Oriental style, on soft cushions before a low ebony-lacquered table.

"Good evening, Dr. Moultron. Please be seated."

When Dr. Sung spoke, his mouth became a gaping

hole in his face. His skin had passed beyond the wrinkle stage, the fat beneath it gone. It had smoothed out and conformed like parchment to his cheeks and jawbone and forehead. The face was gaunt and sallow, like the perfectly preserved face of a mummy. The Chinese silk gown he wore hung loose on his shoulders, as if there were nothing beneath it but bones.

Ansel Moultron sat. "I hope, Dr. Sung, that you will cheer my day."

"So sorry, I fear that we have underestimated the cunning of your esteemed assistant. Tea . . . or something stronger?"

"Tea is fine." The old man poured. Moultron watched the hands, solid as a rock. He hoped he would be as steady when he was a hundred years old, for surely Sung was at least that. "Pletov eluded your people again?"

"Yes. I am afraid the information we received on Turtle Island concerning the girl came too late. We were unable to set up an attempt properly."

"And the woman?"

"She too, I am afraid, escaped." Moultron held his anger in check. "We, however, have identified the man that Pletov met."

Sung pushed a five-by-seven photograph across the table. Moultron examined it.

"An American?"

"Yes. His name is Nick Carter, and he has a very esteemed reputation. That picture, as well as photos of the woman, have been distributed all over this part of the world. Do not fear, Dr. Moultron, they will be found."

"All well and good, my wise friend, but it is Pletov who can derail us. Where is he?"

"He scurries like a swift hare. Friends in Calcutta

believe he was spotted there not an hour ago. Once we see his line of flight, his wings will be clipped. But to other things. The new site is acceptable?''

''Extremely so. The location is ideal and the move was without flaw.''

''Excellent. And when will you need my people to send out your requests for bids?''

''A week. It will take that long to set up the device for demonstration.''

The old man cackled. ''It is amazing, is it not, what lengths great nations will go to, and what great amounts of money they will pay, for a toy?''

Moultron was about to argue that the result of his life's work was far from a toy, when a door opened and a tall, beautiful blond woman entered the room. She bowed to Moultron from the waist, and dropped to her knees beside Dr. Sung to whisper in his ear.

''Splendid. Have the brothers attend to it quietly.''

The woman left.

''Carter and the Djumi woman are in Hong Kong. They were spotted getting on the ferry. We don't know where they are staying, but when they surface . . . I have a thousand eyes in the city.''

''It will be the woman,'' Moultron said, ''who will know how to contact Pletov, where he will be.''

''Do not fear, Doctor, she will be taken alive and she will tell us everything. Remember, it is we Chinese who invented torture.''

FIVE

The driver's name was Chou Lin. He looked to be barely twenty, but Carter knew that meant nothing. If he worked for the Fat Man and Queenie, he was as alert as a fox and deadly as a cobra. The car was a small, four-door Volvo, but from the rumble under the hood it would do anything a Jaguar could do.

They drove through the heart of the teeming city to the newest part of the financial and business section. Chou Lin maneuvered the car into a space alongside a long, wide, glass-fronted, multistory commercial building.

"I shouldn't be more than an hour, two at the most. Cover my ass."

The driver nodded and Carter entered the building. Each floor button in the elevator had a firm designation beside it. Carter pushed number nine, the top floor. Beside the button it read AMALGAMATED PRESS AND WIRE SERVICES, FAR EAST.

The main room was all bustle. There were several people closeted within partitions of translucent plastic that divided and bisected the big main office. Machines clattered, and there seemed to be a constant hum of chatter as people spoke into telephones.

This was the nerve center of the news service. The nerve center of AXE was beyond a door marked WAYNE HARDY, BUREAU CHIEF.

43

Carter went through it into Hardy's outer office. Norma Dailey, Hardy's right hand and an excellent agent herself, was sorting memos and printouts at her desk.

"Hi, Nick," she said, looking up and coming around the desk to meet him. She looked good in a chic, crisp-looking turquoise dress that fit her full figure.

"Norma," he greeted her with a grin. "Do you always work so late?"

"You know better," she laughed. "Only when a hot-shot like you is in town. One phone call and upstairs is tense."

"Wayne's here, I hope?"

"Oh, God, yes, up in the center. Come on."

Carter followed her through Hardy's office and into a hidden alcove where they got into a small elevator.

Ten minutes later they were in the nerve center of AXE Far East, with computers that could get information from all over the world and scrambler phones that could reach anywhere in seconds.

Wayne Hardy spotted Carter from across the room and headed over. Norma Dailey moved past the Kill-master toward a bank of computers. "I'll see if the print-out on Dr. Sung that you asked for is ready."

"Thanks." Carter shook hands with Hardy.

"What's up?" the AXE station chief asked. "No-body knows nothin' and your sheet says you're still in D.C."

"It was a quickie move out. Call set up?"

"Just like you asked, direct line to the big man's private home phone and no taps on the line. You and Hawk planning a coup?"

"Yeah, we're going to take over CBS."

Hardy laughed. "Save me a cushy job when you do. You can take it in there."

Carter moved into one of the glass-enclosed sound-proof cubicles and lifted the phone. "This is N3."

"Yes, sir, it will only be a few seconds."

It was five, and Hawk's cigar-husky voice came on the line.

"Go ahead," the woman's voice said, and there was a resounding click as she backed off the line.

"Give me some good news first," Hawk said dryly.

"I made the meet . . ."

Carter explained in detail and gave Hawk the background he had on Anna Djumi.

"So the bastard wants us to do the dirty work and he slinks back into comfortable retirement."

"That's about it."

"How much?" Hawk asked.

"Fifteen . . . half up front. His copy of the plans on delivery of the second half."

"Where?"

"I don't know. But the woman does. Evidently, after the kill on Moultron, she takes me where we meet again."

"How far can you trust her?" Hawk growled.

"About as far as a file cabinet I see five feet from me," Carter replied.

"Not much to sell the money people."

"I know," Carter said. "My suggestion is, drive it home on the worth of the device. Like Pletov, the bastard, says, fifteen is cheaper than a hundred."

"It means letting the cat out of the bag. A lot of people will have to know. Chances are, word will get to the Soviets."

"They'll know anyway when Moultron puts out his bid requests."

"Any way of knowing when that will be?" Hawk asked.

"None, but I suspect we have at least a few days."

"I'll see what I can do and try to get back one way or the other."

"If it's a go, I'm going to need a team, equipment, God knows what else. I think it would help to clue in Wayne Hardy here."

"Yeah, it would. Go ahead."

"And, sir, if it isn't a go . . what then?"

There was a long pause. "Then we bid like everyone else, but you go after Pletov."

The line went dead and Carter moved back into the big room. Wayne Hardy was waiting for him.

"What's up? World War Three?"

"Close," Carter replied. "Got someplace where we can have a drink, private, very private?"

"I can find one."

"Good, then let's find it. I've got a very long story to tell you."

It was almost two and a half hours before the line got hot again out of Washington.

In that time, Carter told Wayne Hardy everything he knew, as well as everything he could only guess at.

"Not World War Three, but a heavy operation," Hardy sighed when the Killmaster finished.

"Very heavy. We'll know more once I get the site. In the meantime, you can rustle up the basic hardware."

Hardy went to work, and Carter went over the life history and current status of Dr. Chan Lee Sung and his empire.

It was a lot more interesting than Carter would have suspected.

During World War II, Sung was a young dentist in Shanghai, working out of a dingy office in the Lee Po section of the city. From the beginnng, Sung spent very little time in the little office. His real business was gun-running, black marketeering, and opium.

By the time the war ended he was well connected but still not enormously rich. His finances took a downturn after the Communist overthrow in 1949, and Sung fled to Hong Kong.

It was here that Sung's real talents became apparent. A large precentage of his "patients" became "victims," never leaving his office alive.

There was never any bother about Dr. Sung's killings. Most of the deceased were men that the British authorities would have liked to see gone anyway. On the fees from his labors Dr. Sung got back into the opium business, and from there built a criminal empire that spread across the Orient and founded ties around the world.

"Nice man," Carter growled, closing the report.

It was then that Wayne Hardy called him back to the Washington line and Hawk.

"It's a go, N3, but a lot of people are very edgy about that kind of tax money on the street with so little guarantee."

"I can understand that," Carter replied, "but with any luck I hope I can build in a few guarantees. How soon?"

"The Swiss banks open soon, your time. Good hunting."

The line went dead, and Carter hunted up Wayne Hardy. Together they solidified the equipment list, and the Killmaster passed on a list of mercenaries Hardy had used in the past.

"I'll give you the place and the jump-off time as soon as Pletov contacts the woman."

"If it's at least twenty-four hours, there shouldn't be any problem."

Carter headed for the elevator and the street. The car and Chou Lin were not in front of the building. Then, from deep in an alley across the street, a horn beeped once and he saw the lights flick on and off.

He was across the street and fairly deep into the alley before he sensed danger. He stopped, his eyes squinting through the windshield. It was Chou Lin, but there was something odd, very odd.

The eyes, staring, vacant . . . dead.

Carter whirled toward the mouth of the alley.

Too late.

A long black four-door rocked to a halt, blocking off any escape. The driver was a woman, blond. Two bulky Chinese rolled from the passenger doors.

Carter was just pulling Wilhelmina from his shoulder rig when a pair of fists caught him in the center of the back, knocking him the full six feet into a brick wall. Wilhelmina skittered from his hand. Carter took the shock on his shoulder and assessed the situation.

The two were coming in slowly from the mouth of the alley. Evidently they had a lot of confidence in the lone man who had taken Chou Lin.

He was coming at Carter now, lots of teeth showing in a narrow brown face, his hands up and ready.

No weapon.

They wanted him alive.

That, thought Carter, would be their big mistake.

Without a sound, Carter caught him flush on the forehead with the heel of his right hand. The little man staggered, shook his head, and kept coming. He evaded a second blow to the gut and closed.

They fought in a silence broken only by an occasional snarl or labored grunt, cutting and slashing at each other with the edges of their hands.

Carter could see why the other two were holding

back. The little bastard was good, trained, and faster than a striking snake.

The Killmaster weaved and ducked his way out of the pocket and into the open. The man came on again, moving sideways as much as forward, a feather on the balls of his feet.

Carter saw an opening and swung suddenly, hitting him on the point of the chin with a force that numbed his arm to the elbow.

The loner went down and Carter jumped on him, grabbing his hair, banging his head up and down against the cement, then smashing his fist into the surprised face.

Breathing heavily, Carter crawled to the Luger, got it, and whirled on one knee and one foot.

The other two were coming in fast now. Carter got off one shot. The 9mm slug tore the first one's face to pieces, but the second one got to him before he could bring the gun around.

The guy hit him in the side. They both went down and separated. Again Carter lost his hold on the Luger. He got to his feet, but the other man tackled him around the knees. They skidded across the ground and Carter's head banged against the rim of the car's wheel. Stars flew out in all directions, and he felt and heard the thud of a boot against his rib, his shoulder and, finally, with shattering pain, his head.

He crawled under the car to get away from the viciously kicking foot and emerged on the other side boiling with rage. He was halfway to his feet when the man rounded the car and Carter slugged him brutally. He ran headlong into Carter's swinging fist. The attacker literally somersaulted backward. Carter moved to him, gathered the front of his jacket, yanked him to his feet, hit him again, and let him fall.

The guy was down but not out. He was rolling to his side, pulling a big U.S. Army issue .45 from a shoulder rig.

Playtime was over. They had been told to take him alive, but when that failed, kill him.

Carter wasted no time. He let fly with his right foot square in the man's crotch. There was a yowl of pain and eyes disappeared up into a twisting head.

Carter grabbed the .45. Two steps later he had the Luger in his other hand and was running toward the mouth of the alley. The blonde had evidently guessed the show was over. She was already maneuvering the car out. Carter was three seconds late. He managed to get the .45 up long enough to smash the passenger side glass, then the tires screamed and the car lurched away.

Carter fell on his butt. He sat for a full minute to get his wind and unscramble his brains, and then got to his feet.

A bird in the hand, he thought, as he lumbered back toward the two who were still alive.

But they had obviously decided that enough was enough. They were both going over a fence at the dead end of the alley, the one with the crushed crotch being helped by the other.

Carter holstered the Luger and shifted the .45 to his right hand as he pounded after them. He leaped for the top of the fence and got a leg over. Another surge carried his weight over.

He dropped into a black courtyard just as a gun framed, the slug splintering out part of the fence.

Crouching low and running a zigzag, Carter got across the yard and slammed hard into the side of a building. The sound of racing feet made a drum roll in an alley. He caught a flicker of shape and motion against the night sky and aimed a low shot at it, but missed.

He sprinted out of the alley, and saw them dart through light from a doorway. Legs scissoring, arms pumping, he followed around a corner and into a parking lot. He stumbled, but caught himself just as one man turned and got off another shot at him.

The bullet flashed by Carter's head, narrowly missing. But in the instant it had taken the man to fire, Carter gained valuable ground.

He could hear them gasping. Their feet were hitting harder, heavier. They were slowing. Carter forced an extra kick into his own legs, gulped air into his own straining lungs, and moved closer to his prey.

Then they split, Crushed Crotch taking off down another dimly lit alley, the one with the gun down a narrow flight of steps between two buildings.

Carter chose the weaker one and darted into the alley. It came out on yet another parking lot. The guy was waddling along twenty-five yards in front of him. He was heading for the back door of a restaurant.

For all Carter knew there might be reinforcements. He picked up his pace. He gained a yard, another, and then the runner was lurching up a wooden porch toward the door.

Carter's gun-heavy fist caught him in the back of the head. The man snorted and rolled away. Righting himself, he came up with a knife.

Carter drove a foot into his arm and the knife arched away. The man drew back, made a rocking chair of his body, slammed out, and caught Carter in the ribs with both feet. Carter lost his gun. A fist smashed his mouth, splitting swollen lips against his teeth.

He smelled the animal sweat of his prey. He reached

for the throat. The Chinese hooked a thumb into Carter's eye.

The Killmaster drove for the chest, but missed and his head bounced against a tiled post sunk into the wooden floor. A thick miasma of mud rose about his face. He fought free of the other's clutching fingers, came to his knees, and got leverage for a quick succession of heavy blows.

The walled-in porch rocked. A board gave way under Carter, then another, then the floor gave way entirely as the wood collapsed.

The man leaped for Carter's throat. The Killmaster managed to squirm away. The flying body went past him, then there was an agonizing scream followed quickly by the last exhalation from a pair of dying lungs.

Carter whirled.

The jagged edge of the splintered board had passed clear through the man's neck.

"Shit," Carter hissed, crawling out of the hole, "so much for any talk out of you, little man."

He looked around and listened. Nothing but chatter and dishes clattering from the restaurant, and distant street noise.

Quickly, he went through the man's pockets. No identification, but that was normal. Besides some bills, a few pieces of change, cigarettes and lighter, he found a three-by-four-inch headshot of himself.

Looking closely, he recognized the background. From there it wasn't hard to place the blonde in the black four-door as the blonde who had snapped his picture and then run like hell for a speedboat.

He wiped his prints off the .45, stuck it in the dead man's belt, and took off.

Four blocks away, he found a phone and called the AXE hot-line number.

"This is N3, Code Red. Give me Hardy, fast."

The man was on in seconds. "Yeah, Nick, what's up?"

"There's an alley across the street from your building. You'll need body bags and no lights. Just a quiet little cleanup."

"Dr. Sung?"

"Looks like it," Carter growled. "When you get the car cleaned up, deliver it back to the Fat Man. You know where."

"Got it. You all right?"

"Some bumps and bruises, but nothing a double scotch and some sleep won't cure. See you tomorrow."

He hung up and walked another four blocks from the carnage before hailing a cab.

SIX

The Killmaster paid off the cab several blocks from the hotel and zigzagged his way on in. He used a service entrance to the main lobby. The Fat Man wasn't in his usual chair. A sleepy-eyed desk clerk spotted Carter's look and nodded toward a door marked PRIVATE.

Carter moved through it into a dimly lit office. The Fat Man was behind a desk balancing a glass on his paunch. The boy, Charley, hovered nearby on a window ledge. Carter noticed a knife slide back into the boy's sleeve when Carter was recognized.

"You, my friend, have had a dreadful evening."

"That I have," Carter grunted, heading for a bottle on a sideboard. "Your man, Chou Lin, is dead."

"That is sad. His young wife will grieve."

That was it. No mourning wails, no sad lamentations. In the Orient, in the business, it came with the job. You takes your dollars and you takes your chances to make them.

Carter poured himself two fingers, downed it, and poured again before taking a chair across from the Fat Man.

He tossed the photo on the desk. "I found this on one of them." He told the Fat Man about the blonde and the connection.

The Fat Man belched and placed two more copies of

Carter's photograph beside the first one. "There are several of these on the street. I think it would be unwise for you to go out again until you must leave."

"Dr. Sung?"

The big head nodded. "Evidently he wants you and the girl very badly."

Carter sipped and stared into the bottom of the glass until his thoughts gelled. "I want to hit Dr. Sung."

"He is a very unforgiving man."

"So am I," Carter said.

"He has places all over the city, and each of them is practically impregnable. Putting hands on his person would take a small army."

Carter thought some more. "Okay, let's talk about his number one boy and four or five others very close to him. They must play somewhere."

The Fat Man smiled. "A wise decision. A man at play, especially a younger man, tends to think more of his pleasure than his well-being. Charley?"

The boy slid from his perch and wordlessly left the room.

"We will know by morning," the Fat Man said. "I am afraid your dinner with Queenie is canceled . . . the hour."

"No matter," Carter said. "I'm ready for sleep anyhow. What about the woman?"

The Fat Man leaned back, closed his eyes, and recited from memory.

"It is impossible to authenticate what you have already told me of her birth or her parentage. She did come here to Hong Kong from Singapore at about the age of fourteen. For some months she worked the streets, and was then taken into the house of Madame Wo Pong. Evidently she gained many admirers and did very well. One of these, a wealthy shipowner, became quite enamored of her. It was he who helped her escape the country.''

"Escape?"

"Yes," the Fat Man replied. "She hid in a hotel room one night and tried to kill the occupant in his sleep.''

"The man wouldn't have been a certain Ansel Moultron, would he?''

"It certainly was.'' The Fat Man showed a little surprise that Carter would know such a detail, but he continued. "He was here for some sort of scientific convention. He didn't press charges too hard, and her lover got her out of the country.''

"To where?'' Carter asked.

"San Francisco. After a while, he tired of her and she migrated back into her old profession. She appears to have a temper and a bent for homicide. She killed one of her coworkers and fled San Francisco. For a year or more she seems to have moved about the United States under another name. Then she disappeared.''

Carter nodded and crossed the room for more scotch. He guessed that her trek around the United States followed the path of Ansel Moultron, and that her disappearance coincided with his reported death. "Is that it?''

"Not quite. I managed to take a Polaroid of her this afternoon and show it to a few of my closest and most trusted associates. Until a few months ago she was plying her old trade in Kuala Lampur.''

Carter didn't reply. All of it had already fallen in place in his head. If the Fat Man had come up with this much this fast, it was a pretty sure sign that Jerome Pletov had been able to do the same.

"What has she been up to since I left?''

"She went out for about an hour. Charley trailed

along. She spoke to no one other than a few clerks in boutiques, and she never used the telephone . . . either from here or outside. She sent no cables, and she made only a few purchases.''

"Such as?"

"Slacks, boots, a heavy jacket . . . and a gun."

Carter almost choked on the last of the scotch in his glass. "A gun?"

"A snub-nosed thirty-two. Not much for heavy fire-power but very deadly at close range."

"Yeah, and I'll bet that's exactly where she plans to use it."

"The lady knows her way around. Charley almost missed the buy."

"Do you think she was spotted by anyone else?"

"Probably, but Charley is positive she wasn't followed back here."

"Good show. Give Charley my thanks."

"Your thanks have already been included in your bill," the Fat Man chuckled.

"I'll bet they have," Carter said dryly, heading for the door.

"Sleep well, my friend."

He took the elevator up and padded down the corridor to listen outside Anna's door.

No sound.

"Anna, it's me."

"I'm in bcd."

"But not asleep," Carter said.

"Almost. See you in the morning."

He moved to his own door and quietly let himself inside. He closed and locked it before moving to the connecting door between the two rooms. He tried the knob and found it locked.

He turned it slowly, then threw all his weight at the door. He half fell into the room and stumbled across to the bed.

"Damn you . . ."

In spite of closed shutters it was light enough to see her on the bed. She was lying on her back, her black hair spread out like a fan on the pillow.

As he leaned over her, Carter could see the fire in her dark eyes.

"Where is it?"

"Where is what?" She cowered slightly as his bulk loomed over her, but there was still angry defiance in her eyes.

"Give me the gun, Anna."

"You're crazy . . ."

"I know you bought a gun today."

"Go to hell."

He moved toward her cautiously, talking to her, watching her hands. "A snub-nosed thirty-two, to be exact. I want it."

"I'm going to need a gun and I'm going to keep it."

"You'll get a gun when I decide to give you one," Carter said, his voice low, menacing. "In the meantime, I don't want you to own one that I don't know about."

"Go to hell!" she hissed, and rolled to the other side of the bed.

It had been under the far pillow and her hands had moved like lightning to get to it.

Carter raised his left hand slowly and shrugged at the same time, as if in resignation.

"Get out," she said.

He started to turn, then whipped his right hand around. The gun flew across the room and Carter grabbed Anna's wrists.

She broke free.

Making fists of her hands, she fought savagely, battering his neck and face. Blood started to run from his nose, but he held her tight.

"Cool it," he hissed.

"Fuck you!" Suddenly the fingers of one hand clawed for his neck, the other hand aiming for his eyes.

Carter had no choice. He knocked both her arms up with his wrists and then backhanded her. She went over the side of the bed and disappeared.

Carter retrieved the gun and threw it into his own room. By the time he turned, she had crawled to her knees and was staring at him from wide, startled eyes.

"You didn't have to do that." A little blood trickled from one corner of her mouth.

"The hell I didn't."

He helped her to her feet. She staggered a little, so he picked her up and gently laid her on the bed.

"That hurt like hell," she said. "You're bleeding."

"So are you."

She touched the corner of her mouth, looked at her finger and suddenly smiled. "Not as bad as you."

"Well, I'll be damned," he said, lowering his face and kissing her.

To his own surprise, the kiss was tender, making him more than aware of the warmth and softness of her body. Holding his hand, she pulled him down beside her on the bed.

They rubbed noses for a while, kissed again, and ended up chuckling when Carter's nose started putting bright crimson freckles on her breasts.

She sat up straight to touch the blood on his nose and cheek with her fingertips. "I think I really did hurt you worse."

"You did indeed."

This fact seemed to put her in a wonderful mood. She

got up from the bed, turned on the bathroom light, fetched a wet cloth, and wiped his face.

When she finished, she stood with her hands on her hips, the light from the bathroom emphasizing every curve of her naked body. Then she bent and kissed him on the mouth lightly.

"Nick?"

"Yeah."

"Do you always sleep with your clothes on?"

He didn't need an interpreter. Together they got his clothes off, and he pulled her to him until the softness of her breasts were against his chest.

"Do I feel good?" she murmured.

"Yeah, and I'll bet you're going to feel better."

Her long tapering fingers found their way into the hair at the sides of his head. Carter drew her trim, full-breasted body close to him and tilted his head to press his open mouth against the scented softness of her throat. At the same time, he lowered both of his hands to grasp the tight mounds of her buttocks.

"You know what?" she said, her voice a husky rasp.

"What?"

"It's not often I enjoy. Tonight I think I'll enjoy."

"Does that make me duty bound?"

"Hell, yes," she chuckled, "or I'll beat you up again."

He brought his mouth up to her lips, which opened as he neared them. He had a fleeting glimpse of a bright pink tongue that was waiting, and then his mouth closed on hers and he felt her tongue jabbing him and searing him with its demanding fire. His own tongue jabbed in response, then slid and curled around hers. At the same time, he began to rotate her backside, pulling it hard to him and moving it around and from side to side. It set up the desired reaction.

Then Carter went to work with his hand, slowly up the inner part of her thigh. The journey was a slow, thorough one. His fingers took all the time they needed to awaken each nerve beneath the satin smoothness of her skin.

He could sense her mounting arousal. The feel and sight of his own caressing, the move parting her thighs, was having its effect on him as well. He moved his other hand over her shoulder and gently soothed the thrusting hillocks of her breasts.

The fire had spread to both their bodies.

Anna was groaning out loud now. The heat was spreading up her thighs and through her belly. She found it impossible to remain still. Her hips wanted to squirm against him.

Finally her thighs yawned wide and Carter slipped his hand between her legs.

Anna gasped.

He murmured her name as his other hand closed solidly around one of her breasts and squeezed.

"Nick, oh, Nick," she managed to gasp, her voice affected by what he was doing to her. She let her thighs squeeze and release his hand until they were both quivering with delight.

"Yes," he said heatedly, his fingers caressing gently.

"Oh, Nick!" She threw herself against his hand. "Take me, Nick. Please take me!"

That was all Carter was waiting for.

Anna parted her thighs, beckoning him with the beauty of her womanhood. Her knees were up and she wiggled them. Then, as he approached her, she lifted both of her feet high in the air.

He bent first to kiss her thighs, the soft inner slopes of them. He started at one knee and slowly worked downward. Anna pulled at his head, leading him, pressing his mouth more fully against her.

"Oh, yes, that's wonderful," she gasped. "It drives me wild!"

He kissed every inch of her flesh, along first one thigh and then the other. Suddenly he lurched up and forward to kiss the deep navel that crowned her belly.

"Nick, please . . ." she said insistently.

But he paid no attention. Crawling forward on his elbows and knees, he brought his mouth to her bosom. He kissed her breasts feverishly, making a wide circle around one crest and then doing the same with the other.

"Kiss the nipple!" she demanded, grasping her round full breast between her own hands and moving it so that her nipple pressed between his lips.

She gasped and threw her head back against the pillow. It was almost too thrilling to bear. She couldn't stand it any longer. Her belly reached for him. "Go ahead, Nick. Do it now!"

Now she truly could wait no longer. She twisted wildly, settling on her back again. Her long legs took him at the waist and, without further delay, he lanced deeply into her. She cried out and clutched him, thrusting and rotating upward, wanting to feel all of him.

She wouldn't let him use long strokes, as he normally would have done at the beginning. She was too far along. She wanted it to be fast and frantic. Carter followed her rhythm.

Her belly jerked and swiveled as he took her in a storm of unrestrained lust. She moaned and bit her lip and tore at his back.

Carter felt as if he were riding a rocket to the stars. This thrill had been worth all the effort. The rocket soared up and up, seeming to swell and expand as it went higher. And then, somewhere in the trackless reaches of space, the rocket burst apart and shattered.

Carter slept, to awake disturbed.

Passion had overcome common sense on his part. He wondered if it was the same with Anna. Or had she merely reverted to her old trade, this time her pay being his imbalance.

Her head was dark on the pillow, facing him, eyes hidden under a veil of hair. She didn't move as he left the bed. He pulled on a pair of trousers and moved to the windows. When the shutters were open, he stepped out onto the balcony.

In the light from the street he could read his watch. One in the morning. It would be done by now.

The city was a jumble of dark roofs, splashed with yellow where lamps burned against the approaching fog. The air was heavy with a hundred smells.

"What are you thinking?" came her voice from the bed.

"That there are a hundred of Dr. Sung's people out there hunting for us. They tried for me earlier tonight."

"Why didn't you tell me?"

He thought he sensed genuine concern in her voice. "I'm telling you now. The quicker we get out of Hong Kong, the better. The money is in Pletov's Swiss account by now. How is he going to verify with you?"

"An ad in the *Ho Ching* Chinese-language daily."

"That can't be done until day after tomorrow. It might be too late."

He came back to the bed, sat, and started to light a cigarette. Anna stirred, shaking her face free of the blue-black hair. Then her hands came up to meet behind his neck, pulling him down to her.

Unwilling, Carter shrugged himself free. "Do you trust me, Anna?"

Silence.

He sat on the edge of the bed, conscious of her firm leg against him, knowing that she was watching him. She was waiting for him to speak again and he had nothing more to say until she answered.

Then she touched his wrist with her fingers. They were no longer cool, but hot, imprisoning his wrist.

"I trust you."

"Then where's the new testing laboratory location? We can't wait two days."

He could feel her body tense, then relax. She pulled and he stretched out beside her.

"Halfway between Singapore and Kuala Lampur, in the jungle near Muar."

"Thanks." He paused. "Is Moultron really your father?"

"Yes."

"Do you really want to see him dead?"

"Yes."

No change in tone. No rise in inflection. Just a calm statement.

It was ten in the morning. Carter came instantly awake and slid from the bed.

"Must you?" Anna mumbled.

"I must, and you must, too. I'll send down for breakfast. I don't think it wise that we go out."

In his own room he grabbed the phone and dialed Amalgamated's number. He gave his code designation and Wayne Hardy's. A minute later the man's sleep-groggy voice came on the line.

"I take it you've got a cot in your office."

"Yeah," came the reply, "but I only got to use it for an hour."

"How are we doing?"

"Better than I expected," Hardy replied. "The standard equipment is about put together. I should have a team by noon today, all hand-picked."

"Good enough," Carter said. "I've got a jumping-off place . . . Singapore."

"Ouch."

"Can you do it by noon tomorrow?"

"I think so. You need transportation, too?"

"Yeah, very private. I'll need some specials."

"Like what?"

"A sampan and jungle gear."

"No problem. We've got some good contacts down there."

"Check with you later." Carter killed the connection and dialed the desk. He ordered breakfast, and then the Fat Man himself got on the line.

"I have news."

"Have coffee with us," Carter said.

"Twenty minutes."

Carter used the shower, shocking himself with cold water. Then he dressed. On the bed, the small Browning he had taken from Anna gleamed up at him. He checked the loads, walked into her room, and dropped it on the bed.

He was halfway back to the door when she walked out of the bathroom. She glanced from him to the bed and back to Carter.

"Now we trust each other," he growled.

The boy, Charley, wheeled in a breakfast cart and left. They were down to coffee when the Fat Man joined them.

He sat down, poured coffee, and rolled his eyes

Anna's way while readying a cigar. Carter got his meaning and nodded that it was all right to talk in front of her.

"You're in luck," the Fat Man said, "if that's what you want to call it. Do you know the House of Nine Moons?"

"No," the Killmaster said.

"I do," Anna said, stone-faced. "It's in the hills near the border. It's owned by Dr. Sung but run by an Englishwoman named Lorelei."

The Fat Man nodded. "Generally it caters to wealthy businessmen from Hong Kong and Kowloon, or high-ranking officials from the north sneaking over the border for a night of fun."

"It's a whorehouse," Carter said.

"Please, please, my friend. The House of Nine Moons is a pleasure palace. All the girls are Caucasian, brought in from America, Australia and Europe. Very high class, and very expensive."

"All right," Carter said, "what interest do I have in the House of Nine Moons?"

"Two or three evenings a week, on the slow nights, the girls are obliged to entertain free of charge."

"Dr. Sung's chosen few?"

"Exactly," the big man said, nodding. "If their habits run true to form, tonight will be one of those nights."

Anna's eyes whirled from the Fat Man to Carter. "You're mad! I've seen that place. It's guarded like a bank vault to keep out the undesirables."

Carter smiled. "I think of myself as very desirable."

"What are you going to do?" she asked, her eyes telling Carter that she already knew.

"I'm going to let Dr. Sung know that he's got a tiger by the tail."

SEVEN

The House of Nine Moons was actually a compound made up of one huge, pagodalike structure and several outbuildings. They had been set down in the middle of a single patch of thick woods. Around the whole perimeter was a high wall. Outside the wall on three sides was vast, open, rocky ground. On the fourth side was a tin and tar-paper shantytown with dirt streets and musky cooking odors.

A quarter mile to the north was the frontier of China. Due south was Hong Kong and Kowloon.

Carter had set out just about dark on a motor scooter, dressed in baggy Chinese pajamas, a black wig, and a coolie hat. At a spot prearranged by the Fat Man, he had hidden the scooter and meandered his way through the villiage to the house of Tuang.

The old man was a retired thief, and looked like Confucius incarnate. Three of his daughters worked inside the compound as serving girls. One by one they padded by Carter, each of them imparting as many facts about the main house and the outbuildings as she could.

Old Tuang himself supplied the last word. "There will be fourteen visitors this night to the House of Nine Moons. Only eight will be of interest to you. These men will be entertained in the west wing, as they always are. The other guests will be in private suites on the lower level."

There was no mention of the reason for Carter's request for assistance, nor any curiosity expressed about his intent. The tall man with the strong eyes and gruff voice had come to Tuang from the Fat Man. That was reason enough, and the old man wanted to know nothing else.

Leaving them, Carter walked to the north until he was on ground high enough to survey the whole of the compound and the single, winding road leading to the gate facing south. Here there was an addition to the main wall, a large square jutting out with a parking lot in its center. The outer gates were electronically controlled and watched over from a small blockhouse gussied up like a pagoda.

Inside the blockhouse were two men with submachine guns. Two more men, in tuxedos with bulky bulges under their jackets, greeted the visitors and parked the cars. Inside the first gate, the visitors were shifted from their cars to a canopied carriage and driven through the second gate on up the winding road to the main house. The second gate, like the first, was watched by four men, all armed.

It would be a rare undesirable who would gain entrance through either of those gates. Exiting without permission would be just as difficult. Both gates were heavy forged steel, reinforced with drop bars that went into three-foot concrete holes when they were closed. Nothing less than a tank could get through them.

Carter had expected such precautions, and allowed for his own escape another way.

Through the night glasses, he watched car after car arrive. By ten-thirty, the reservations were filled. Lights were on all over the main house, and even from such a distance he could hear music and, now and then, loud laughter.

Their party had begun, and now it was time to start his.

Low clouds were drifting across the face of a pale half-moon as Carter made his way back to the village. Silently, stooped and shuffling, he made his way past candlelit windows and openings with bamboo curtains for doors. He passed few people and none of them gave him a second glance.

Between the edge of the village and the rear of the compound was about thirty yards of open ground and a narrow, rutted road. He paused, staring across at the formidable wall silhouetted against the night sky. It looked discouragingly high.

His watch read exactly eleven as he sprinted across the open area and dove under the line of low shrubs at the base of the wall.

He didn't have long to wait. A jitney pickup with dim amber lights came around the edge of the village. Somehow it found the road, and turned toward Carter to rattle and bump along in low gear. The road was so narrow that in a couple of places one set of the car's wheels ran off into the softer mud and the engine had to roar to free them.

The old truck coughed to a stop, and a wiry little man dressed in black emerged nimbly and trotted to the rear. By the time he had unloaded a black canvas bag and a grappling hook and line, Carter was at his side.

Wordlessly, Carter shed the pajamas and the coolie hat. Beneath them he wore a black turtleneck and skin-tight black trousers. The black, soft-soled sneakers from the bed of the truck replaced his sandals.

The little man was already pulling equipment out of the bag. As Carter blackened his face and tugged on a pair of black driving gloves, the diminutive Chinese armed him.

A bandolier of spare 9mm clips went around his shoulder. A utility belt of plastique cubes, detonators, timers, and flash-fire grenades went around his waist. Also on the belt was a commando knife and a silenced artillery pistol with a thirty-two-round drum magazine at its butt. All the rounds had been cyanide-dipped. Over it all went the sling of an American M3 sub-machine gun with a sleeved barrel to act as an effective silencer.

When Carter was ready, the little man—still without uttering one word—climbed back into his truck. As the Killmaster glided back into the shrubbery, the truck backed around to face the direction from which it had come. Just before pulling away, the driver gave Carter's darkness a jaunty wave that was almost a salute.

Carter shuddered at the noise the old truck made departing, but he knew it wouldn't matter. If there were walking guards on the other side of the wall, they would never suspect an intruder to make so much racket.

The Killmaster waited a full five minutes after the sound of the jitney died away before going to work. Then he bent to the line and grappling hook. He laid the coils neatly over his left forearm, and gripped the line with his right hand about two and a half feet from where it was attached to a ring on the foot-long shaft.

Lazily, Carter started swinging the weighty hook in a head-to-toe arc, his eyes on the very top of the wall. Slowly he increased the speed. When he let fly, the three hooks sailed upward, only to glance off the stone a foot short of the top.

He dodged as the hook fell back. It landed on a flat stone, shattering the stillness and forcing Carter to wait another few minutes in the shadows before a second try.

When he was sure it was safe, he re-coiled the rope, swung the hook again, and launched it. The prongs glinted momentarily in the moonlight before the hook disappeared over the top of the wall.

Success.

Carter pulled it gently, gathering in the slack. It slipped slightly, held, and the line grew taut. He tugged, testing, but there was no more give. He pulled harder, going so far as putting his toes on the side of the wall and lifting himself completely off the ground.

The hook was lodged solidly.

He was about to start step two, when he heard a motor and then saw two bright headlights round the corner of the compound two hundred yards to his left.

It was a jeep with two men in the front, the hourly patrol around the exterior perimeter of the compound. Either they were early or he had taken too much time.

The lights were turning his way. There was no time to disengage the hook. Unslinging the M3, Carter dove under the shrubbery and sweated.

The jeep had almost reached Carter, when it suddenly veered to the right, leaving the road and jolting over the open ground into the village. It disappeared for a few seconds and then reappeared, coming to a stop in an alley between two rows of shacks.

The lights were gleaming directly at Carter's area and the rope dangling down the wall.

The Killmaster held his breath and slowly raised the muzzle of the M3. With any luck he could get them both, dispose of the bodies and jeep, and still have time to get in and get out before someone ralized they were missing.

Then the lights went out. He heard two car doors slam. He could barely make out the two figures moving toward the door of one of the shacks. There was a sharp rap, solid, like the butt of a gun on wood, and then the scraping noise of an ill-fitting door being opened.

The two smiling men were bathed in dim light. One of them said something, which was quickly followed by feminine giggles.

Carter sighed with relief, put the safety on the M3, and slung it back over his shoulder.

It didn't take a genius to figure out that the boys on the bottom rung of Dr. Sung's organization wanted their own brand of fun and games with the fair sex.

The door squeaked shut, blocking out the light, and Carter went back to work. He took two turns of the line around his forearm and started walking up the side of the wall. It was easier than he had expected. The uneven surface of the stone let his soft-soled shoes get a good grip.

Near the top, he paused. No glass, no spikes, and there didn't seem to be anything that looked like a sensor.

He muscled himself on up and lay flat along the wall, feeling with his hand until he found a place to plant the hook after reversing it. From there it was a simple "walk" down the other side, where he flipped the rope up and down until it came free and fell at his feet. Quickly he coiled it, attached it to his belt, and moved off through the trees along the wall.

It was about fifty yards before he found what he wanted: a fairly clear path through the trees from the general area of the house to where he stood. It was narrow, but wide enough for a small car, and the ground was fairly solid.

From the belt he took eight cubes of the plastique, unwrapped them, and began molding them against the wall. He went from the level of his head to his knees, spacing the blobs about three feet apart. This done, he inserted detonator/receivers in the blobs and activated them.

Then he jogged inward about thirty yards and set up the beam transmitters in trees, one on each side of the "road" he would use. Then, very carefully, he activated the beam between them.

This done, he melted back into the trees until he found a gravel path leading toward the first of the outbuildings around the main house.

The path he was on meandered and eventually skirted a pond. Carter followed it, and came up on a small cottage. In his mind he clicked off what he had been told. This one would be the sleeping quarters for the guards. He bypassed it and jogged on, being careful to avoid clumps of dried leaves.

Then he saw his first strike, a narrow, flat-roofed building with three car bays and one smaller door between two of them. This would be the garage unit for the cars used by the woman—Lorelei—the doctor, and other VIPs in the organization.

Cautiously, Carter approached the bays. He tried each door in turn and found them all locked. Under his breath he cursed when the walk-in door was locked as well.

As quietly as possible he went to work on the door with a pick. Seconds later it opened and he slipped inside.

There were two big Bentleys and a small, sleek Mercedes coupe in the bays. In the rear of the garage—which was evidently the shop area—a late-model Cadillac sat with its ass end jacked up and all four doors gaping wide.

Methodically, Carter moved among the cars in the bay. He removed the keys from the two Bentleys, bent them out of shape, and discarded them. Then he suction-cupped two flash grenades to the gas tanks of each of them. The keys to the Mercedes, he pocketed.

The Cadillac didn't look as though it would move, but he started for it anyway, to place two more flash grenades.

Three steps from the car, his foot scraped a can. The car rocked slightly, and up out of the back seat of the Cadillac came a sleepy-eyed Chinese mountain in dark blue coveralls.

One look at Carter and his rig and the mountain was moving, getting bigger and bigger and even starting to erupt in a roar. Had it been the Cadillac itself, Carter thought, it couldn't have looked bigger.

The Killmaster had no time to get the pistol out or unsheath the knife. He had no time to do anything but sidestep the giant's crouching lunge. Even then his shoulder caught Carter in the gut, jackknifing him and sending him sailing back into a row of grease barrels.

The clatter was like Fourth of July fireworks, and the big man kept coming. Carter was half down, his back on the top of the barrels. He teetered there, groped for the knife, planted both feet against the diving man's chest, and shoved.

Tried to shove.

The guy was big and he was fast. He was also as hard to knock over as a sixteen-wheeler semi rig.

He grunted, grabbed Carter's leg, and tried to spin him like a top. When the knife came up, he swatted it out of the Killmaster's grip as if it were a fly.

Carter managed to check the hulk and even move him back a couple of feet. This gave him space to roll off the barrels. As he did, the big man swung wildly. Carter went under it and planted his fist wrist-deep in the other's gut.

It was supposed to bend him, setting him up for a shot at the beefy slab of his jaw with the Killmaster's knee.

It didn't.

It stopped him, whooshing air, but that was about all. He took a breath, swung, and missed Carter again.

But he didn't miss the Cadillac. His fist smashed through one of the side windows. He roared with pain, and blood streaked what was left of the glass on both sides.

Carter moved in, but the big man's free arm came around like a log with an anvil on the end of it. He caught Carter on the side of the head and sent him spinning.

The bloody fist was extracted from the shattered window. Suddenly he was looming over Carter, a tire and wheel rim lifted high above his head.

To himself, Carter said, "The hell with it," and drew his gun.

Three slugs spit from the end of the silencer to stitch across the broad chest. He cried out like a bull bellowing, and blood spurted toward Carter from the three wounds.

The tire dropped behind him and the giant crumpled to his knees. But, as he did, he grasped the rising Carter around the middle.

"Shit," the Killmaster hissed, amazed at the man's resilience. He smashed the gun barrel against the side of the giant's head until the octopuslike grip around his middle weakened. Carter then brought the barrel down across the front of his skull and he fell away.

Carter sagged against the Cadillac. The huge Oriental was down but he wasn't out. And he wasn't dead.

Slowly the man crawled to his knees. His bloody hand fished around the floor and came up with a tire iron.

"Enough is enough!" Carter rasped.

He raised the pistol, pumped five more slugs into the lurching body, and it was over.

Quickly, Carter ran to the door and peered through the small pane. No one was stirring.

He planted the two grenades on the Cadillac's tank and dragged the mountain away behind some barrels. The pool of blood on the floor was partially disguised by three handfuls of grease rags. Then he unlatched the bay door in front of the Mercedes and slipped out the walk-in door, relocking it behind him.

Other than the buzz of insects and the music and laughter from the house, the night was still calm.

Keeping in the shadows of the outbuildings and ornamental trees between them, he moved toward the rear of the mansion. The moon was coming and going now behind the clouds, giving an eerie feeling to the area that helped rather than hindered Carter's movement. He became just one wavering shadow among many.

Far to the rear of the house he came to an ornamental wall and went on tiptoe to peer over it.

There were terraces from the wall all the way up to the house, graduated in size and elevation until they reached a large veranda leading to huge glass doors with lights behind them.

That was out.

He looked up. About half the windows on the second story were lit. Luckily, a two-window room in the west wing corner was dark.

Carter went over the wall and moved in a crouch across the first terrace. He went over a second, lower wall, and came up short.

In front of him, covering almost the whole expanse of the second terrace, was a gigantic pool. Two naked women were lolling in the shallow end. Just above them, at the foot of a flight of stone stairs almost as steep as an upright ladder, was a man lying on a chaise.

The stairs led up to the house level and the big glass doors. The man was stretched out watching the cavorting women. Carter was debating, retreat or kill, when a third woman—a tall, statuesque blonde—came down the steps.

The Killmaster recognized her at once. He had seen her three times before. The first time in a bikini, just like the one she now wore. The second time was behind a camera, and the last time behind the wheel of one of the Bentleys he had just booby-trapped.

That wasn't too surprising. What startled him was when he heard the man address her as Lorelei. It brought a smile to Carter's face.

With any luck, he thought, he would get many birds with just a few stones.

Lorelei exchanged a few words with the man and then the other two women. Carter didn't hear all of the conversation, but guessed the gist of it when all four of them padded up the stairs and into the house.

He crouched and waited. Three minutes later a light came on in the center of the house, second floor. The blonde appeared at the window and pulled some drapes.

Carter made note of the room's location, and took off for the wall and the corner of the west wing.

From the top of the wall to the eaves of the roof was about thirty feet. He made the hook secure on the first try. The walking climb up the side of the house was a little more difficult than the wall had been because of the smooth surface. Carter sweated out every foot, fearful that someone else would decide to take a late-night swim.

At last he was over the ornamental façade and on the roof. He was breathing hard by the time he made it, and moved carefully. There was no slope to the roof, but loose tiles were a constant threat. Carefully, he shifted the hook to a spot above the dark balcony and attached it. As quietly as possible, he lowered himself. The second he touched, he secured the line so it wouldn't wave around, attracting attention, and opened one side of the doors.

It was a large, single-room suite on two levels. To his left was a sitting area. To his right was a door with light showing through a crack beyond it. Directly in front of him was a bed. On it was a long-limbed brunette who was dead to the world.

When Carter reached her, he knew why. Alcohol was heavy on her breath. Nevertheless, he could take no chances. From the smallest pocket in the utility belt he took a self-contained hypodermic. He broke the tip and slid the needle into her arm.

There was a small groan. Other than that she went further out. Gently, he tucked her under the covers. The women working for Lorelei and Dr. Chan Lee Sung weren't his targets. If possible, no harm would come to them.

The Killmaster moved to the door. Behind it he could hear a shower running. Gripping the pistol, he opened the door and stepped into the bath. Through the shower curtain he could see the outline of a man.

On tiptoe, the Killmaster moved to the shower. With one motion he whipped the curtain aside and placed the muzzle of the gun just behind the man's right ear.

Two slugs removed the side of his head and Carter closed the curtain.

Past the bed and on the lower level, he cracked the door. The hall was empty.

Carter moved across it and barged into the opposite suite. It was like the first, and he was on the lower level.

A short, fat man in a robe was fixing a drink at the wall bar. At the sound of the door he turned, right into the barrel of the pistol.

The man clenched his fists and stared at Carter in confusion. But he wasn't seeing the Killmaster. For perhaps a full five seconds he was paralyzed.

Then on his fat face grew a look of sheer horror, of utter disbelief. His mouth sagged open, his lungs expanded, and he let out a weird, low, wailing sound.

Before the sound became a scream Carter shot him, twice in the head.

A quick search of the suite told him that that man had been without female companionship.

He dumped the body behind a sofa and ran down the hall to the next suite. It was empty.

Loud music came through the door of the next one.

A man was at the window across the room, his back to Carter. He jerked his head around as the Killmaster entered. He wore a Beretta in a shoulder rig, and had it out in the blink of an eye.

Carter shot him twice.

The man crumpled slowly, hands coming up toward his chest and his knees bending before they buckled. Even when he fell, he didn't go all the way down. He stayed in a sitting position, one hand pressed against the carpet. He hadn't let go of the gun, but he couldn't quite get it up.

When he tried, Carter kicked it away and shot him twice more. This time the cyanide-tipped slugs worked.

Carter sensed movement to his left, on the upper level of the suite. He was running before he even saw her rolling out of the bed. Before she could scream, Carter's hand was over her mouth.

"I don't want to hurt you. Nod if you understand."

She nodded.

"I am only interested in Dr. Sung's people. There were supposed to be eight here tonight. Are there?"

Again she nodded.

"All right, besides your friend here, where are the others? I'm going to take my hand away. If you speak in anything above a whisper I am afraid the gun in your belly will go off. Do you understand that?"

Again she nodded, and Carter cautiously removed his hand.

"M'Gawd, man, who are ya?" Her accent was thick Cockney.

"I'm the original bad ass, lady. Talk."

She rattled off the location of the three kills Carter had already made. "They's four of 'em playin' in the double suite down at the very end of the 'all."

"Playing?"

"Gamblin', some Chinee game with big dice."

"Are they alone?"

"Prob'ly not. Chances are one o' the girls is hangin' around servin' 'em drinks . . . they're drinkers, they are."

"Double suite . . . tell me about it."

She did.

Carter made some mental calculations. "Okay, where's number eight?"

"That'd be Moo Liang. He's with Lorelei. She always takes care o' Moo Liang. He's a bit weird . . . but then so's she."

"What do you mean, weird?" Carter asked.

"He don't never do nothin', neither does she. They both like to watch girls."

Carter nodded. That would explain the little scene he had witnessed at the pool with the two naked girls.

"Get a robe on."

"What fer?"

"Like I told you, I don't want to hurt any of the girls if I can help it. We're going into the second suite down the hall, and you're going to get your girl friend in the clear."

She didn't object but grabbed a silk, kimono-style robe and shrugged into it.

It didn't surprise Carter too much when they passed the body on the lower level and her only reaction was a calm comment: "Gar, ain't he a bloody mess."

Again the hall was empty. They slipped into the first of the two suites. It was empty, and through a crack in the connecting door Carter checked out the second room.

Four men sat around a table in a haze of smoke. A tall, bored redhead sat at the bar nearby.

"Go get her. Tell her you need her help for a minute . . . anything. But don't say a word to any of them, understand?"

For emphasis he holstered the pistol and unslung the M3.

"I got ya, mate. It's yer war."

She moved into the other suite and approached the redhead. They exchanged words, and without even looking at the four men headed back Carter's way.

He was ready with the hypodermic when they came through the door, the redhead last. She barely had it closed when Carter buried the needle in the fleshy part of her shoulder and she sagged against him.

" 'ere now . . ."

"She's fine, only asleep. Grab her feet—let's get her on the bed."

The woman obliged, and Carter applied another

hypo. When they were both sleeping soundly, he killed the lights and snaked open the door.

The first one didn't look up until Carter was only five feet from the table.

The Killmaster started with him and moved methodically around the table. From that range, the slugs—even without being tipped in cyanide—would have done the job.

He emptied a full magazine and then checked each of them to make sure.

Not a breath in the bunch.

He killed the lights, locked the suite with the bodies from the inside, and exited through the other suite.

Seven down.

One—and Lorelei—to go.

EIGHT

Carter reentered the hall and counted doors. It was no good. The center of the house where he had seen the blonde, Lorelei, at the window was at a mezzanine level, between the first and second floors. The only way he could reach it was down a wide stairway, which would expose him to anyone in the huge rotunda between the massive front entrance and the dual stairways leading off to the two wings.

A cautious peer around a wall at the top level told him the worst.

Two of the tuxedos stood by the door in an at-ease position. But there was nothing at ease about their manner. They were alert to every sound. If Carter went down the stairs, they would spot him before he hit the next landing.

He was about to settle for seven out of eight, not leave a calling card, and retrace his steps to the roof and the grappling hook, when Lorelei emerged from a side room and approached the two men.

After a few words, one of them moved out of sight under the stairs. The other exited through the front door, and Lorelei started up the stairs.

Carter dropped to the deck and against the wall, watching, hardly breathing.

Lorelei might have been a bit kinky, but she was all woman. She had long, smooth, tanned, shapely legs.

The shimmering green gown she had changed into from the bikini revealed them as she walked; the dress had slits on both sides up to her thighs. Her hair was long, honey-blond, and contrasted vividly with her delicately tanned face and wide blue eyes. Her mouth was wide but well formed, and her whole carriage exuded confidence and poise.

As she grew nearer, Carter was able to notice what he had missed before. It was in the eyes, the set of the mouth, and the slight flair to the nostrils: a cruel hardness he'd seen all too often in his career.

The Killmaster let a sigh of relief slip from his lungs as she moved across the landing without glancing his way. She disappeared through an unseen door, and just before it closed he heard a male voice.

Bingo. All the rest of the eggs were in the same basket.

He was about to slip down the stairs, when one of the tuxedos reappeared balancing a tray. He moved up the stairs with the tray in a perfect position so he wouldn't see Carter intercept.

By the time he did, it was too late.

"Pssst," Carter hissed, lifting the tray and leveling the gun.

The guy had guts. He was still going for the revolver under his coat when Carter shot him through the heart.

Carefully, the Killmaster set the tray on the floor and lifted the body as a shield in front of him. Without knocking, he moved through the door.

Evidently the little party was over. A tall Chinese with a hard, scarred face sat on a settee in the center of the room sipping a glass of wine. The blonde was posed above him smoking a cigarette.

The tall man, Moo Liang, went for a gun beneath his

coat the instant he saw blood on the tuxedo and Carter's bulk beyond the corpse's shoulder.

"Don't," Carter growled, pushing the body forward and putting a round between the dead man's legs. "Take it out nice and slow with two fingers and drop it on the rug. That's it. Now kick it this way . . . not too hard."

The tall Chinese did as he was told, but his eyes kept moving, looking for an opening. The woman hadn't moved. She stood, calm and cool, even taking an occasional drag on her cigarette.

"You know, of course, that you'll never get out of here alive," she said in a low husky voice that was far from the Betty Boop delivery Carter remembered from the island.

He smiled as he picked up the revolver and shook out the shells. "You can bet your ass, lady, that if I don't get out alive, neither will you. Move a few feet that way, lie down, and spread out."

She flicked the ash from her cigarette and didn't move. Carter raised the pistol and carefully aimed.
When she still didn't move, he put two slugs between her legs right through the dress.

She dropped the cigarette and dove for the floor. She spread wide to four corners as Carter turned to the man.

"You are the American, Nick Carter."

"That's right," Carter said, turning him around. "If you know that, you know I'll kill you. Now, let's talk."

"I have nothing to say."

"Maybe not," Carter replied, steel in his voice, "but when the lady sees what I do to you and knows that she's next, she'll talk."

Carter rammed the barrel of the gun into the small of Moo Liang's back and kept his voice low. "I want Dr.

Sung. Where can I find him?''

"Only those closest to Dr. Sung know where he sleeps.''

Carter grabbed an earlobe and twisted it savagely. "And you are one of the closest.''

"You are a dead man," Moo Liang said.

The woman moved. Carter put another slug inches from her head. She squealed in terror and lay still.

"You are scum, Moo Liang. You know everything and everyone in Hong Kong. You would sell your sister for a dollar. You know who slept where for the past twenty years. I mean to kill Dr. Sung. Where is he?" For emphasis, Carter kicked the man in the ankle, sending him to his knees.

Carter put a shell in the chamber of the revolver, spun the cylinder, and placed it on the floor near Moo Liang's hand. Then he stepped back and leveled his own gun.

"I give you the same chance you give your victims, Moo Liang, before you dump them in the bay. Where can I find Dr. Sung?"

"You are a pig, Nick Carter."

"Pick up the revolver, Moo Liang."

The Chinese snatched up the gun. He cocked and fired in a single motion.

The hammer clicked on an empty chamber, and Carter put a single slug dead center in his forehead. By the time he had toppled to the floor Carter was crouching over the woman, fishing a hypo from his belt.

"Lorelei, is it?" She nodded. "Tell Dr. Sung I'm coming for him. Tell him I'll be in his shadow very soon. Tell him that his death will be slow."

"You're . . . you're not going to kill me?"

"Of course not," Carter growled, jabbing the needle

in her arm. "I want you alive, as a messenger."

The powerful drug worked in seconds and she was sleeping soundly. The Killmaster holstered the pistol and jacked a new clip into the M3.

The hallway and stairs just outside the suite were empty. But the second tuxedo was standing just inside the front door smoking a cigarette.

There was no way around him. The moment Carter stepped out onto the landing he would be seen.

He swung the door wide, walked to the edge of the landing, and started down. Surprisingly, the tuxedo didn't look up until Carter was nearly to the bottom. His eyes went wide, his mouth dropped open, and his right hand headed under his jacket.

Carter dropped him with a stitching burst across the front of his chest. The Killmaster stepped calmly over the body, opened the front door, and started down the steps.

The old carriage driver took one look and threw his hands in the air, flattening his back against one of the high spoke wheels.

"Do you have a gun, old man?"

"No . . . no, I swear!"

"I have no war with you. Run, that way."

The old man took off as if he were a teen-ager. Carter crawled up onto the high seat, took the reins, and clucked the horse into movement. He was across the courtyard and fifty yards from the garage, passing one of the smaller buildings, when a door opened and a man stepped out. Carter put a burst along the wall above his head and the man jumped back into the house.

Carter maneuvered the carriage right up against the door, jumped down, and ran.

The bay door in front of the Mercedes glided up

easily. He pulled the pins on all the grenades and started up the powerful little sports car. Then he stepped back and emptied the magazine across the windshield. The butt of the M3 did the rest and he had a clear field of fire from inside the car. He readied a fresh clip and started the Mercedes.

Just as he roared out of the garage he saw men spilling out the side window of the house. Two short bursts sent them diving into the bushes, and Carter put it to the floor.

Then World War III started.

The grenades went off in the garage and the gas tanks quickly followed. It was a quick-spreading fire. In seconds the whole compound was bathed in an orange glow. Men were running everywhere, firing at anything that moved including the Mercedes.

Carter drove directly toward the inner gate, the barrel of the M3 spitting slugs over the hood. When the magazine went dry, he laid it on the passenger seat and threw the last of his grenades.

If everything wasn't already mass confusion, it was now. About fifty yards from the gate, the Killmaster down-shifted and threw the wheel hard to the left. The car swung around facing the way it had come, with the rear wheels spinning, screaming for traction.

Out of the corner of his eye Carter saw two figures running toward him. By the time the face of one of them appeared at his side, Carter had his gun back in play.

The face became hamburger and disappeared. The second figure was in front of the car trying to bring an assault rifle up into firing position. The nose of the Mercedes sent him flying before he could get off a shot.

Carter retraced his route fifty yards, spotted the narrow lane, and cranked the wheel hard to the right. He bumped and jolted over the rough ground, twice bouncing the side of the car against trees.

He was close to praying under his breath as he hurtled toward the two trees and the trip beam. Already the wall was looming like a stone monster before him.

If for some reason the trip beam didn't work, he and the Mercedes would be an accordion against the wall.

He passed the point of no return, and then the blast erupted. He felt the shock wave and saw smoke and flying rock. For a second, he thought the opening wouldn't be big enough.

It almost wasn't.

He hit it at sixty miles an hour, and the scream of metal tearing off the sides of the car against jagged stone set his teeth on edge. Three quarters of the way through, he almost ground to a halt.

"Shit, shit, shit," he growled, and dropped the Mercedes into its lowest gear. The tachometer needle went crazy. Carter dropped the clutch when it sounded as if the engine would burst from beneath the hood, and the car shot through.

He turned right on the perimeter road and was through the gears by the time he hit the front corner of the compound. As he slid around the corner, he rammed a fresh clip—his last one—into the M3 and poked the barrel over the dash.

Twenty yards short of passing the outside gate he started firing, and kept it up until he hit the main road and turned left.

He discarded the M3 and checked the rearview mirror. They had the front gate open and two jeeps were already roaring through after him.

That was all right. He had expected it.

The jeeps would be no match for the Mercedes's

speed. In fact, there was little likelihood that they would come anywhere near Carter by the time he hit Hong Kong.

But that wasn't the plan. The Killmaster wanted one more coup.

It was nearly a mile to the sharp, uphill "S" curve. Halfway through it, he braked to a quick, sliding stop, leaving the Mercedes sideways in the narrow road. Quickly he leaped out and plastered the last block of plastique to the driver's side door. He jammed an impact detonator into the glob and took off.

A shallow ditch paralleled the road on his left. It wouldn't conceal a man. Thin, scraggly trees were just beyond the ditch. They were bordered by a few low bushes displaying tiny, withered yellow blossoms. The other side of the road was even worse. There were wide-open fields without a ditch or a fence. The fields didn't look much different from the dusty road itself. It was a water-short, semibarren area.

The element of surprise wasn't going to be as much in his favor as he had hoped.

He started toward the spindly trees in a running crouch. He wasn't even off the road when the first pursuing jeep whirled around the curve, sliding to the extreme outside of the road.

Carter stopped, raised his arm, and sighted on the center of the windshield.

Just as he started firing, the second jeep rounded the curve, coming full bore.

It was made to order.

The windshield of the first jeep shattered, blinding the driver. It hit the side of the Mercedes full tilt. The explosion lifted the jeep high in the air, and it hurtled over what was left of the burning Mercedes.

The second jeep's driver tried to evade, but it was too late. He hit the front of the Mercedes, went up to teeter on two wheels, and then slid into the open field on its side.

Carter emptied the rest of his gun's drum magazine at anything that moved in or around the jeep, and took off.

If any of them were still alive and not crippled, there would be no fight left or taste for further pursuit.

He hit the last of the curve and climbed about thirty feet into the rocks.

The motor scooter was just where he had left it.

Quickly, he cleaned his face and slid into a light jacket. When the utility belt was shed, he climbed onto the scooter and carefully tooled down the rocky incline. When he hit the road he pushed the little machine to its maximum, fifty miles per hour.

Forty minutes later he was climbing off the scooter in a hangar on the corporate side of Kai Tak Airport. Wayne Hardy and the Fat Man, rolling a cigar between thick lips, awaited him.

"Since you're here," the Fat Man said with a wide smile, "I assume everything went well?"

"Not a hitch," Carter replied. "Dr. Sung will have a very bad day tomorrow." He turned to Wayne Hardy. "The woman?"

"She's already on the plane. Your goods will be arriving tomorrow night. Your contact is Bernhard Graff. He's a German importer. The stuff is coming in through Taiwan as textiles. Here's a number where he can be reached. You are Jonathan."

"Jonathan," Carter repeated. "And the men?"

"They come through Graff as well. Don't worry, he's dependable."

Carter nodded and turned back to the Fat Man. "Tell Queenie I'm sorry I wasn't able to make dinner."

"The lady understands."

Carter shook the big man's hand, clapped Hardy on the shoulder, and jogged toward the sleek corporate jet.

NINE

Getting through customs and immigration was no problem, even with Wilhelmina and the rest of Carter's tools in a briefcase. Singapore is a financial center and a bustling trade metropolis. Business is king and businessmen have a lot of clout.

Mr. and Mrs. Jonathan Longtree of Atlanta, Georgia, were passed through with barely a nod and no question of passports.

The safe house was in a new high-rise apartment building overlooking the bustling docks. This was good, too, because the docks were Graff's bailiwick. They were barely settled in when Carter called the number Hardy had given him.

A secretary answered. "Who is calling, please?"

"Jonathan."

"One moment, please."

It was closer to three before a husky voice spoke in a thick accent. There was no greeting, and the tone was abrupt. "This is Graff. Your goods will arrive this evening at Pier Three, aboard the *Mali Four*."

"About what time?"

"The dock space will be cleared by ten. I presume the *Mali Four* will arrive shortly after that."

"I'd like to have the sampan before then, if possible.

I don't want to warehouse."

"That is understandable. Do you know Singapore?"

"Moderately, but my companion knows it quite well."

"Good. Do you have a car?"

"Yes."

"There is a fishing village just east of the city, called Poo Loob. Drive there just after dusk. Once you reach the village, it should be no trouble locating the school."

"School?" Carter asked.

"Very convenient and quiet. The leader of your group is an Indian. His name is Sankjab."

Graff went on to give Carter detailed instructions on the meet with the Indian and the eventual transfer of the goods.

"I take it I won't be meeting with you."

"No," the man replied. "I am watched closely. It would do neither of us any good. Good hunting, Jonathan."

Carter hung up and checked the suite that would be their home for the next few hours.

It was a spacious studio, one high-ceilinged room in two levels. The bedroom area, with a bath off of it, was on the upper level. The area where Carter stood was furnished with rich but subdued heaviness: jewel-toned carpets, deep chairs upholstered in wine-colored velvet, Chinese ginger jar lamps and modern art on the dark walls.

Two doors in one wall pulled out to make a bar. He was just building a scotch when Anna appeared on the upper level. She had pinned her hair up and changed into a slinky, sexy robe that made him stare.

"Something wrong?"

"No," he replied. "I just like what you do to clothes
. . . any clothes. Drink?"

"A gin." She came down to get it. "I would like a
bath. Do we have time?"

"We have all day, until nightfall."

She sipped the drink. "Then it's a bath for me." She
moved back to the upper level and paused at the bathroom door to look back at him under heavy-lidded eyes.
"It's a very large tub . . . more than big enough for
two."

Carter smiled and saluted her with his glass as she
ducked out of sight.

He returned to the phone and dialed Hardy's private
number at AXE Hong Kong.

"We're in."

"Any problems?"

"None," Carter replied. "I contacted Graff. The
goods are safe. I have a meet with an Indian named
Sankjab tonight."

"A good man," Hardy said. "Even though he's
strictly a mercenary, your dollar buys his loyalty. You
may be surprised when you meet him."

"How so?"

"He's a dwarf," Hardy said with a chuckle. "But
don't let that bother you. He can do ten times what a
normal-sized man can do."

"What about the detailed maps?"

"They'll be in the invoice packet with the goods."

Carter sighed with relief. Everything thus far seemed
to be going like clockwork. "What's happening at your
end?"

"It looks like your little party at the House of Nine
Moons did some good. Dr. Sung's people are turning

Hong Kong upside down looking for you. The word is that he's so mad that he's even forgotten about the woman. He just wants your head.''

"Good,'' Carter chuckled. "Let's hope he keeps looking in Hong Kong for the next forty-eight hours. What about Pletov?''

"The bastard's good. Our people had a line on him from Bombay to London, but he gave us the slip.''

"I figured he would. He's done too much planning on this. My guess is he's already in Switzerland, in a very safe hole. But keep trying.''

"Will do. When do you jump off?''

"If all goes well, tonight.''

"Good luck.''

"It'll take one hell of a lot more than luck, but thanks.''

Carter hung up and walked up the few steps to the second level. He could hear splashing and Anna's voice humming from the bath. He nudged the door open.

She was right. The tub was very large, big enough for five people. She was on her back, her sharp breasts floating on the top of the water, her head slightly over the side with her eyes closed.

Carter lounged against the wall and sipped his drink while letting his eyes feast.

"You're staring at me.''

"I'm a man.''

"I know.''

"We'll get detailed topography maps tonight with the goods. Are you sure you can pinpoint the new laboratory compound?''

"Positive, within five hundred yards. Did you make contact?''

"Yeah, an Indian named Sankjab.''

Her eyes opened. "I don't trust Indians."

"We'll have to trust this one. He's got the boat, he runs the crew, and he knows the territory."

"Do I get to take my gun?"

Carter laughed. "That's what I gave it back to you for." He finished his drink, debating the next question. Anna sensed it, and raised her eyebrows expectantly. "Besides revenge, what do you get out of this?"

"Security," she said softly.

"How so?"

"From Pletov. One million dollars."

"And you trust him to pay you off?"

"I have no choice."

"What if he doesn't?" Carter asked.

Her eyes went dead. "I searched years for Moultron. I can search years for Pletov."

Carter wasn't surprised at her answer. "You'd kill him."

"Yes."

"Bloodthirsty little thing, aren't you?"

"No more than you. I heard you tell the Fat Man and the other one at the airport what you did at the House of Nine Moons."

"Touché," Carter said with a tight smile. "We make a good bloodthirsty pair."

She pursed her lips, then shot the tip of her tongue out to moisten them. "It's a luxurious tub, isn't it?"

Carter got her meaning, and stripped. The water was hot and soothing. So soothing that he lolled for a full ten minutes before moving closer to her.

For another ten minutes they did the usual things a man and a woman do together in a bathtub, then Carter picked her up and carried her into the bedroom. Dripping wet, he deposited her on the bed and joined her.

"We're making a habit of this," she whispered, moving against him.

"Oh? We're husband and wife, remember? Isn't this what husbands and wives do?"

Teasing, for what seemed like an hour but was only minutes, with each of them trying to outwit the other.

Then, with mutual growls of urgency, Carter rolled between her quivering thighs. She was ready, guiding him, and he entered her smoothly, bringing a groan of joy from both of them.

"You said we have hours," she whispered.

"Yes."

"Then take hours."

And he did, knowing that by the same time the following day they would both regret it.

It was just after seven, and total darkness had set in by the time they reached Poo Loob. It was the difference between night and day. Where tall buildings, bustling people, and gaudy neon signs were the norm of the big city, Poo Loob, in contrast, was dark and quiet. Not even a streetlight could be seen.

There were no docks, piers, or wharves. Small fishing boats were pulled, bow first, up onto the sand. Around them fishermen worked by the light from fuel oil lanterns preparing nets for the night's work.

"Where do we find this schoolhouse?" Anna asked.

"Somewhere . . . up there," Carter said, turning.

There were only two roads: a paved, two-lane one running parallel to the ocean, and a dirt lane going inland toward low hills.

"Look for a cross," Carter said. "It's an old, burned-out missionary school."

Carter had to concentrate on the road. It was an effort to keep the tires out of the deep ruts and try to avoid as many of the deep potholes as possible.

About five minutes later, Anna spoke. "There, off to your right."

Carter saw it, a tall cross jutting into the night sky above a two-story cinder-block building. He geared down, turned into an even narrower lane, and jolted over rocks and debris until they pulled into an open area that had once been some sort of playground.

The headlights of the car flashed across the fading whitewash of the walls, cutting the night briefly, not decreasing the blackness but accentuating it.

"I don't like this," Anna whispered.

"Sometimes you have no choice. You have to fly a little blind."

He switched off the motor and headlights, and the darkness enveloped them. He turned in the seat, looking at the old school building, cinder-block walls with glassless windows and empty doorways. There was no sound or movement other than a soft breeze coming off the sea behind them.

Carter checked Wilhelmina's loads and slipped from the car. "Watch my back. Any movement, anywhere, honk the horn and then cover yourself."

Anna nodded and he moved off.

The upper story, the ceiling, doors, windows, and furnishings, had been ruined long ago by the fire and water and stripped by scavengers, but the cinder-block walls had been left intact.

Inside, nothing remained but a cement floor. Everything else—every door and beam and nail and windowpane—had been hauled away.

Inside the shell it was darker than outside, the walls shutting off most of the moonlight.

Carter pressed his back against the wall, Wilhelmina cocked in his right hand. "Anybody here?"

"It depends on who you are looking for." The high-pitched, hoarse whisper came from above Carter, near one of the windows.

"My name is Jonathan."

"Splendid. Step out where I can see you."

"Kiss my ass," Carter said.

"Ah, a cautious man. I have always said, a cautious man is one who can be trusted."

Suddenly Carter saw a figure drop from somewhere above him. It hit, rolled, and came up on its feet dead center in a spot of moonlight beaming through a hole in the ceiling.

"I am Sankjab."

Had he been six feet or more he could have played linebacker for the Rams. As it was, he was about four feet even, with arms and legs like posts and a torso to match. He was everything in miniature, except for the Uzi submachine gun held carelessly in one hand.

Carter stepped forward until he, too, was in the light. He pulled his jacket to the side and holstered the Luger. "Shall we talk?"

"Fine," the little man chuckled. "Step into my office."

Carter followed him down a flight of steps and into a windowless room. From a knapsack on the floor he produced a small lantern. "Close the door."

By the time Carter did, the lantern was lit and a bottle of feni—a potent Indian liquor made from the juice of cashews—along with two shot glasses had appeared.

The little man sat and the Killmaster joined him.

"Drink?"

Carter nodded. "If it will facilitate business."

"Good. You have money?"

"Lots," Carter said, accepting one of the glasses.

"Even better. I make it a policy never to drink or do business with a man who doesn't have money."

They drank and Carter managed to keep his jaw clamped not to show the other man his pain as the throat-burning mouthful hit bottom.

"Good feni, eh?"

"Damn near as good as paint thinner," Carter croaked, holding out the glass for another pour. "How much did Graff tell you?"

"That you need at least five men, all capable of doing what four can do. That you need a reliable boat. And that you are planning a small war somewhere north of here in the jungle."

"That's about it," Carter said, nodding. "Can you fill the bill?"

"Can you pay five thousand per man plus five for the boat?"

"I can."

"Then the bill is filled. When do we go?"

"Tonight, if possible. The hardware is coming in on a freighter, the *Mali Four*."

"Singapore?"

"Yes," Carter said. "Pier Three, sometime after ten tonight."

Sankjab nodded and thought for a moment. "It would be better to off-load ship to ship—fewer customs problems if the goods never touch the docks."

"I should think Graff can handle that."

More thought, and then the little man leaned far forward, until his wide face was near Carter's. "There is

word all over this part of the world about a man much
like you.''

''Oh?''

''Dr. Sung has put a price of one hundred thousand
American on the head of this man.''

''Is that right?'' Carter said.

''One hundred thousand is over twice as much as
thirty thousand, is it not?''

''It is.'' Carter pulled his shirt from his pants and un-
buckled a money belt. He laid it out in front of Sankjab.

The Indian ran his hands lovingly over the leather,
and chuckled. ''It is a pity Dr. Sung was not first with
the cash.'' He looked up at Carter. ''You will need a
boat, a small launch. It will be safer to pick you up at
sea . . . at least outside the main harbor.''

''You name the place.''

From under the leather vest he wore, Sankjab produced a small map. ''Shall we say, three A.M., about
here, just off Seskait Island?''

''Fine.''

''One other thing . . .''

''Yes?''

''The woman that two of my men are now entertain-
ing in your car . . . she will be accompanying you?''

Carter laughed. ''She will.''

''The jungle is very dangerous, hard on a woman. She
will not slow us down?''

''I think she can take care of herself.''

Sankjab stood. ''Then we have a bargain.''

He extinguished the lantern, repacked the knapsack,
and they mounted the stairs. Outside, Carter bit his lip
to keep from laughing out loud when they walked to the
car.

Two men stood, one on each side of the car, their legs spread wide. Their hands gripped each other's tightly over the hood, and Anna sat on the front of the roof, calmly smoking a cigarette while the muzzle of the Browning moved back and forth to cover the two men.

"You didn't honk," Carter said.

"I didn't need to," she said and grinned, then glanced down at Sankjab. "Do they belong to you?"

"They do," the little Indian said, unable to suppress a smile himself.

"You should teach them that some women do not docilely do as they are told."

It was nearing midnight, cooler now and less humid with a steady breeze off the sea. Carter took a deep breath and raised the binoculars to his eyes again.

Six hundred yards down the waterfront before him, Sankjab's sampan nestled beside the *Mali IV* like a feeder fish to the side of a shark. They had been loading for nearly an hour, and Carter could tell from the speed of movement and the diminished size of the crates that the operation was nearly finished.

From this distance and in the darkness, Sankjab's craft looked like any other plying the harbor. But its exterior appearance was deceiving. Its hold was larger and its bow a little more streamlined for speed. Like any other sampan, it had a single mast with a mainsail and an oar tiller.

Deep in the bowels of the craft was the main difference: a 350-horsepower diesel marine powering twin screws. Another added accoutrement was a hand-operated, pulley-lift, four-by-four elevator built into the mat-covered top of the crude cabin. When it was raised, the bottom section held two men manning a pair of Browning .50-caliber M2 machine guns.

Steps on the walk behind him brought Carter around. It was Anna.

"How is it going?" she asked.

"They're about through. You?"

"A small inboard over there in the commercial section of the marina. His name is Sing Loo. He'll take us anywhere around the outer islands for a hundred dollars American."

Carter nodded. "Anything funny?"

She shrugged. "I think I'm paranoid. I'm beginning to believe everyone looks at me funny."

They waited another fifteen minutes. When Carter saw Sankjab's crew securing the forward hold hatch, he dropped the glasses to his chest.

"Let's go!"

While the harbor was alive with movement and the sound of foghorns and claxons, the marina was like a tomb. The only sound was water lapping at the sides of moored boats.

"You didn't tell this Sing Loo what we are doing, that we're meeting another boat?"

"Of course not," she answered. "I told him we were lovers who wanted to see the outer islands in moonlight."

Carter followed her along a worse-for-wear pier past small craft of all shapes and sizes. A few, not many, sported lights in their small cabins, and the air was heavy with the smell of rice and fish that had been cooked earlier for the evening meal.

She slowed. "There, on the end."

It was a twenty-five-footer with a small cabin amidships. A single mast with its sail furled swayed back and forth as the incoming tide rocked the boat. Two fifty-horse outboards were mounted on the stern. They were lowered in the water and their covers were off. A dim light shone through the closed curtains over the single starboard porthole.

"It's awfully quiet," Carter said.

"Hang back," Anna murmured, moving forward. "I'll raise him."

Just off the bow, she stopped and called out in Chinese. It was a full minute before a shaggy head popped out of the hatch, saw Anna, and flashed her a toothless grin.

"Your gentleman friend, missy?"

Carter slipped the Luger back into his shoulder rig and stepped forward. "Right here. Are we ready to go?"

The tip-off was the little Chinese man's eyes. They took in Carter and then darted to the tall bow of the boat tied next to his.

"Nick, look out!" Anna cried.

Carter started to roll away, tugging Wilhelmina as he moved. He didn't see the figure sailing through the air because he was all in black against the darkened part of the sky.

But he felt the feet, one to the side of his head and the other up, under his arm, crashing against his elbow.

His arm turned numb. The Luger skipped away, and Carter sailed through empty space. He bounced off a pair of fuel drums and tried to regain his feet. Something chopped him across the neck.

He spun, reaching, and grabbing only empty air.

Boats, pier, and sky turned end over end. He landed hard on his shoulders, breath gushing from his lungs in a rush. A heel drove viciously at his throat, and he was barely alert enough to roll dizzily away from it. The second try caught him on the side of the jaw and red lights flashed in his head.

Through sound more than sight, he knew that there were at least two or them and Anna was trying to handle the second attacker.

Grunting, he pawed at the rough planks of the pier and came up, shaking his head, trying to push the red spots out of his eyes. The edge of a rough palm lanced into his throat.

Carter swayed on his knees, sucking through the bright, hard agony that wouldn't let the air pass. The face floating over him was out of focus, hazy, leering at him with an evil lopsided grin.

Carter wobbled up and stuck a fist at it, felt a hand snap around his wrist, felt himself yanked off-balance, and knew something painful was on its way.

Then he was free, rolling on the pier but without a hand on him. He spat, pumped a gulp of head-clearing air into his chest, and forced his eyes to clear.

A tall, angular Chinese all in black was on his knees, both of his hands vainly reaching over his shoulders trying to tear away the tiger on his back.

Anna was riding him as if he wore a saddle. With her strong legs fastened around his middle she had the fingers of one hand firmly entwined in his hair, jerking his head back. The other hand was raking at his eyes and face, and her clawing fingernails were already dripping blood.

Carter forced the rest of the mist from his eyes and moved forward. Gasping for breath, he twisted the fingers of his left hand in the man's turtleneck. Squealing with rage, his blind eyes nothing but crimson sockets, the Chinese struck at Carter. But as Anna dropped from his back he suddenly had no leverage.

The Killmaster pulled him off the deck and wrapped his right hand around an ankle. Then, holding him in midair, he swung in a complete circle. At the end of the arc Carter hammered his head against the side of the larger boat.

There was a howl of pain. Since there was still life, Carter swung around again. This time he heard the skull crack and dropped the body. Then he stepped over it to Anna where she stood holding his Luger in one hand and her Browning in the other.

"Where's the other one?"

"There." She pointed with the Luger. A body was floating facedown between the two boats in the water. "I shot him . . . with your gun."

Carter nodded. That was why he hadn't heard a shot. The Luger was silenced.

"Who were they?" she asked.

"Dr. Sung's people, maybe. Where's the boatman?"

"I don't know."

Carter went over the rail, motioning her to follow. At the opening of the hatch he stopped. "Tell him to come out."

She did, in Chinese. Nothing.

Carter went down the steps cautiously, filling his left hand with the penlight.

He found the boatman cowering under a pile of dirty rags and a blanket in the corner.

"Get up! Do you speak English?"

"Yes, yes, English . . . bad men, harbor *foo payong.*"

Anna came down the ladder. "*Foo payong* . . . that would be like a mugger."

"Hard to believe," Carter growled. "They were too

good, pros, and they wanted to take us without any noise."

"Yes, no noise," the Chinese said, chopping the side of his hand to his own neck. "No noise, rob you, throw body in bay. Bad men, Vietnamese *foo payong* . . ."

He rattled off a lot of rapid-fire Chinese in a dialect that Carter couldn't understand.

"What was that all about?"

"He claims they prowl the waterfront by day dressed as students. They spot rich Europeans and then hit them at night. It's done all the time. They took the fifty dollars I gave him, and threatened to kill him if he warned us."

"Do you believe him?" Carter asked.

"I think so."

Carter used his left hand to squeeze the boatman's mouth open. Then he pushed three inches of the Luger's silencer into the cavity.

"Ask him if he still tells the truth."

Anna spat out the words and the man garbled a reply.

"He swears on the ashes of his father and the heads of his sons. I believe him, Nick. It was just bad luck."

"Let's hope so," the Killmaster hissed. "We'll have about one more day for a surprise at the compound, but not if Moultron knows we're in Singapore." He freed the old man. "Now tell him to get this scow moving!"

TEN

Carter flipped his cigarette over the side and leaned back against the wheelhouse. Behind him, on the aft deck, he could hear the snores of Sankjab's men. The little Indian himself and one man were handling the boat.

It was nearly dawn now, and they were about thirty-five to forty miles out, tacking gently north under sail.

They had cruised under diesel power for the first hour or so after he and Anna had come aboard. During that time, he, Anna, and Sankjab were in the tiny cabin poring over maps by the light of a lantern.

Anna hadn't let them down. She could read a map, and in no time had drawn coordinates and pinpointed the site of the new laboratory and testing ground.

"You are sure?" Sankjab asked.

"Positive," she replied firmly. "It's an old rice plantation. At one time a rich colonial owned it. Dr. Sung purchased it many years ago, and had it refurbished as a processing plant for illegal rubber smuggled in from Burma and lower Malaysia. When the price of rubber went to hell, he converted it to an opium processing plant. It is well fortified, and the fields around it are planted in rice as a cover."

Sankjab bent over the maps, doing calibrations. He

worked for several minutes before leaning back with a sigh.

"Fifteen miles south of Muar. We dare not take the Muar road inland from the beach."

"Walk?" Carter asked.

Sankjab nodded. "The only way. Two of my men know this country well. It is all rice field and jungle, dotted like a chessboard."

"What do you suggest?"

"We lay off the coast about forty miles and run north with the wind. About noon tomorrow we head in, about here. We'll be fishing all the while, so there will be little suspicion aroused among the locals."

"Overland, with packs," Carter said, "how long will the march take?"

"I would say twenty-four hours. With some rest, that would put us near the compound some time in the evening, day after tomorrow."

"That long?" Anna exclaimed.

The Indian's broad face broke into a wicked leer. "It will be, how you say, no joy-walk. The jungle is heavy. And even though it is not monsoon season, there will be swamps and some irrigated rice fields we will have to cross. Also, we should stay out of sight as much as possible."

"Whatever you say," Carter said. "It's your neck of the woods."

"Very well. I sugest the two of you go up on deck and get some sleep now while it is cool. When it is light, you will have to say down here and it will be much too hot to sleep with any comfort."

He had given them two bedrolls and they had come topside. Carter had set them up against the wheelhouse bulkhead and sat down. Anna had taken her cigarettes and moved to the bow where she now sat, leaning slightly over the wooden rail.

She was dressed in a thin shirt that stretched tautly over her breasts, a pair of knee-length shorts, and bush boots. Her long black hair had been up, but the wind had loosened it so that it now flowed over her shoulders to cascade down her back.

"Are you going to sleep at all?"

She looked back at him, perfectly calm and steady. "Pretty soon, maybe. How's your neck?"

"Sore as hell. Worried?"

"No." She turned back toward the sea. The moonlight did nice things to her face and body. He imagined her on an evening outing in Paris in silk and diamonds, with other women cutting her with jealous eyes.

Somehow it didn't wash.

He remembered something she had murmured before, just after making love and just before falling asleep. *No one ever cared if I died in silks of consumption or rags of malaria. I see no reason to worry about it now.*

Carter crawled into the bag and tried to sleep.

The sun was high and hot. They were less than a mile out and running on the diesel. Anna was still below. Sankjab was at the wheel. His four men were hauling in empty, slitted nets. Carter was on the bow, a pair of binoculars to his eyes.

"Anything?" Sankjab called out.

"Port's clear, starboard's clear," Carter yelled back. "Where the hell are you going in?"

"That dark spot just to starboard," the Indian replied, already keeling over.

The Killmaster sighted the spot and felt the morning's

rice do a little flip-flop in his belly. The water was just clear enough to see a sandbar under the surface, and the "opening" Sankjab was aiming for looked like a solid wall of jungle.

He turned. "You do know what you're doing?"

The little man threw his head back and let out a high-pitched cackle. "Have faith, my friend. I've been getting away from gunboats in these waters for twenty years! You'd better drop to the deck—we will be getting a bit scraped topside."

The bow surged as Carter looked back toward the jungle shoreline looming larger and larger before them.

Then he dropped to the deck as heavy vines, tree limbs, and giant spider webs enveloped the boat. He heard the first scrape of the keel over the sandbar, and then the craft lurched to port, sending him rolling in that direction.

It seemed they stayed that way—the bow half in and half out of the water—for an eternity. Actually it was only a few seconds, as Sankjab dropped the drive shaft into a lower gear and the old diesel roared in response.

Suddenly the boat righted, surged ahead, and they were through the wall of jungle and in a large lagoon. Sankjab idled back and Carter started to rise.

"Don't move." It was one of Sankjab's men, standing right between Carter's legs.

"What . . . ?"

"Don't move!"

Carter lay still.

Suddenly the blade of a bush knife came down less than six inches from Carter's side.

He looked.

Four feet of headless snake wriggled in spastic death throes across the deck. "Snake," the man said.

"I can see that," Carter replied, fascinated by the ugly, dismembered head opening and closing its fanged jaws at his shirt.

"Very bad snake," the man said, sticking the head with his knife. "Poison the shit out of you." He picked the still writhing body up with his hand, threw both parts into the water and calmly walked away.

Then they were moving under cover of a thick canopy of trees, groping deeper and deeper into the jungle. Finally the engines stopped and an anchor was dropped.

Sankjab came forward. His men were already busy lowering two small skiffs into the water.

"This lagoon is completely hidden by silt and jungle. The boat will be safe here. We'll take skiffs inland as far as possible. There's a village, that way, about a mile. We'll have to avoid it."

They both went aft. The hands were uncrating the supplies. Wayne Hardy had assembled quite an array. One man would carry a big Bren machine gun with ammo. Another was already strapping a Stinger surface-to-surface rocket launcher on his back. A small crate containing ten missiles would be carried between the two men. All the rest of them had sidearms and Thompson submachine guns with bandolier belts containing extra clips. A second crate held plastique, detonators, hand grenades, and communications gear.

Anna joined them and, without a word, started pulling on a pack. Carter smiled. Like the rest of them, she was now dressed in shapeless jungle camouflage fatigues.

"How far inland can we go in the skiffs?" she asked Sankjab.

"Two miles, maybe a little more," the Indian replied. "Get in!"

The heavy air was like a wall of heat as they paddled inland. The stream was narrow and barely moving, each side bordered with thick undergrowth. Both of the small boats were seriously overloaded, making their progress slower than it would have been otherwise.

Still, Carter thought, looking from side to side, it was better than hacking through the jungle.

The stream split, and following Sankjab's lead, they took the narrower of the channels. It was even darker, with trees overhanging the water, leaving visible only a center strip of sky above them.

They traveled nearly an hour, and then hit a bridge. It looked more like a dam because of the solid mass of vines that had grown across it.

"This is it," Sankjab said. "Beyond here the stream is too narrow and shallow for the boats."

Carefully, they stepped out. The water was only knee deep and scarcely moving. Among the growth under the bridge they located a natural tunnel to hide the skiffs. This done, one of the men handed out machetes to each of them.

Toting the packs and the heavy hardware, they hacked their way through the vines and thick growth to the top of the grade. There they found a natural passageway and moved out.

"This is an old path used between villages," Sankjab explained. "But no one will likely be on it in the heat of the day."

On each side the new growth was dense, often reaching above their heads. After about a mile, they came to a small clearing and Sankjab called a halt.

He dropped his pack and glanced at his watch, then took a bearing on the sun.

"This path will take us to the upper paddies. Once there, we can follow the edging paths around the village."

"It will be dark in about three hours," Carter said.

"That's right," Sankjab agreed.

Carter glanced around at the thick jungle, hoping that there would be more open rice paddies than jungle if they were going to move in the dark.

He looked at Anna, and could tell from the wide-eyed expresion on her face that she was thinking the same thing.

They traveled steadily for two hours. The footpath broadened so that here and there harsh sunlight found them. They came to an open area overgrown by weeds nearly as high as a man's armpit.

Again Sankjab called a halt. He crouched, motioned Carter to his side, and parted the weeds.

"There."

Carter peered through the opening. He could see skeleton frames of huts and large areas of earth that had been recently dug out for fresh paddies when the monsoons came.

It was a large village, with palm-leaf bungalows on the high ground and huts on high stilts where the ground was low and swampy.

"Do we try now?" Carter asked. "In daylight?"

"No," Sankjab replied. "Chances are Dr. Sung has a watcher or two in each village. If they spot anyone who isn't a native heading in the wrong direction, they probably send a runner. It was common practice in the opium days, and there is no reason to change it."

"We wait, then?"

Sankjab nodded. "Until after dark."

They spread out around the clearing, Sankjab and the others falling asleep immediately.

Carter settled in beside Anna with his back against the cool bark of a tree.

The stars were just coming out as they moved in a single line around the village. A half hour later, the group was on the other side.

The uplands had been fairly dry. As they left the village and moved down, their nostrils detected the wet, sour smell of a water hole.

"We will refill our canteens here," Sankjab said.

"Is it safe to drink?" Carter asked.

"Of course," the Indian shrugged, holding up his empty canteen and dropping three malaria pills into it.

At this time, before the onset of the monsoon, the water hole was an area of trampled mud, with only a trickle of fresh water coming from under a ledge. The bones and hair of oxen, mired from previous rainy seasons, could be seen here and there, accounting for the bad odor of the place.

But the water was clear and cold.

Sankjab moved in beside Carter as they filled their canteens. "We were followed as we passed the village . . . no, don't be startled."

The Killmaster remained calm, filling his canteen and reattaching it to his belt. "What now?"

"We continue. Takbar will drop out in the darkness and handle the problem."

They moved on. The footpath was soon joined by other footpaths to become a fairly wide jungle thoroughfare.

Carter didn't know where the lead man, Takbar, left

the party, but an hour later he was back in front of them.

Sankjab fell back until he was at Carter's side. "The problem has been taken care of."

"And will it be drawing flies?"

"Of course not. Takbar buried it in the newly soft ground of the paddies. He will make good fertilizer for the next year's rice crop."

Carter nodded, grim-faced, and picked up his step.

They pushed on through the night, fording a winding stream several times and passing another, smaller village in the darkness.

Just before dawn they came to a wide, deep gorge. Across it was a narrow, swaying bamboo bridge that arced deeply down into the darkness.

"I don't like this," Anna whispered.

"Nothing we can do," Carter said, taking the lead. "We can't fly over it."

Its initial downward steepness proved even more unnerving than its bob and sway. Carter didn't make the mistake of going slowly. He walked right on, not looking at the abyss, not even at the narrow footway, but at the closing lines of its perspective far in front. By degrees the drunken feeling of the first steps left him. He grew in confidence; he even experienced a giddy sense of pleasure from the sensation of dangling in space on spider webs. Then he was in the middle, deep between the walls.

He could sense Anna right behind him following directly in his footsteps, and hear the others behind her.

"You all right?"

"Of course I'm not all right," she hissed. "I'm scared to death. But for God's sake don't stop."

They started up, which was twice as difficult. Steeper and steeper it got, but at least they all made it, winded and sweating.

Carter then looked back and down. "Will we have to come back over this?"

Sankjab nodded. "Perhaps very swiftly . . . if we are pursued."

Carter's eyes met the little man's gaze head-on. No words were needed.

The answer to pursuit was to leave no one alive to pursue.

By dawn they hit open country, rice paddies with only stray patches of trees dotting the landscape.

"We will stop here," Sankjab announced. "The compound, if you are right, missy, will be about five miles farther on . . . that way. We will sleep most of the day."

They found places to stretch out as the gray of dawn turned the sky to orange.

Carter dropped beside Anna, who was sitting cross-legged on the dry ground, combing her hair. She looked up at him through her hair and kept combing it. It was very glossy and fell like a satin veil to her shoulders.

"Preparing for battle?" he chuckled.

She returned his smile. "In my own way."

"Like I said, you're a bloodthirsty little thing."

The smile faded and her face set in hard lines.

"Carter, you haven't even seen the real me, yet."

ELEVEN

They waited until it was good and dark before breaking down the packs and distributing the extra explosives and ammunition.

It had already been decided earlier that they would move as close as possible to the compound and then halt again. Carter and the big Malay lead man, Takbar, would then run the perimeter to get a set on the buildings and try to get a count on Sung's men.

"It shouldn't take much more than an hour, hour and a half at the most," Carter said, adjusting the Thompson slung over his shoulder.

Sankjab nodded. "If you are not back in two hours, we leave."

Carter smiled. "You're all business, little man."

Takbar took the lead and they moved out, staying as much in the shelter of the jungle as possible, and staying out of the bright light of the moon. About a mile from the compound, they could see the paddies begin.

"Must stay low now."

Carter nodded and fell to his elbows and knees. Even with the soft ground it was slow going, and painful for every muscle in the body.

The big Malay appeared to thrive on it, and Carter summoned the energy to keep up.

The edging paths through the paddies seemed to run in every direction, and Takbar seemed to be taking them all. Far ahead, Carter could see the main gate of the wood and wire enclosure. For several minutes it seemed that they were heading right for it, then Takbar would turn off in another direction. Around and around they went, up the successive flat levels of the paddies.

At one time there must have been a small village strung out where the paddies now existed. Now and then abandoned native huts thrust their palm-thatched gables into silhouette against moonlit clouds.

Twice Takbar stopped and pointed at the ground in front of them. Each time the Killmaster had to strain his eyes to see. Certain sections of the edging paths had been booby-trapped with land mines.

"They don't like visitors, do they," Carter commented dryly.

"Maybe many more up closer. We get in paddy."

Moving through the two-foot-deep water was much slower, but eventually they could hear people, voices, and the dissonant sad melody of a man singing to the accompaniment of a guitar.

"Look there!"

Carter looked. He could see small spotlights glowing atop the fence, pointed inward. They were spaced every hundred yards. Larger, more powerful spotlights faced outward. They were dark now, but Carter knew that if any alarm were given, they would be lit and the spot where they were currently kneeling would be daylight.

"Steadily, quietly," Takbar whispered, and they slithered ahead.

They were less than fifty feet from the fence when a dog barked and ran up to one of the chain-link sections.

Both of them dropped to their bellies, most of their

bodies submerged in the water. Neither of them breathed.

No one investigated, and in a few minutes the dog left.

"This way!"

They moved to the right, past a long wooden panel of the fence, and stopped at another chain-link section.

It was only twenty paces to the wall, but an impossible twenty paces. The ground was smooth, cleared down to the grass blades. Beyond the fence they could see guards walking the interior perimeter.

Carter timed one of them, and guessed a two-hundred-yard section when he saw the guard turn and walk back.

"I'd say eight on the wall," Carter murmured.

Takbar nodded. "Probably two night shifts to stay alert. They wouldn't have armed guards out in the daytime. Too much curiosity for passing natives."

"Good thinking," Carter said. "I'm going to get a closer look."

Still on his belly, he moved forward again until he was only a couple of feet outside the fence.

He counted the huts—four large, two small. He guessed these were barracks for the guards, probably a kitchen, and maybe a small sleeping hut for any native servants.

There were only two large buildings. One was obviously the old plantation house. It stood in the rear of the compound by itself, with lights ablaze on the wide veranda that ran all the way around its four sides.

The other building was very long—over four hundred feet—in the center of the compound. It sat high on pilings that lifted it as much as fifteen or eighteen feet from the ground.

From it, Carter could hear the steady *thump, thump, thump* of a diesel generator. He could also see huge insulated pipes running from the compound wall into the buildings, and hear pumps moving the water.

And the building was new, not more than a few months old.

That would be where they were testing the device, and where Moultron would eventually demonstrate it, Carter figured.

Before oozing back into the paddy, he had to find out one more thing. Cautiously, he eased forward and rolled to his back. He stared long and hard at the wires leading to one section of lights.

Just as he suspected, the insulation was rotting and had worn away in some places. He was about to move out, when he caught sight of a second set of wires running from the light stanchion down to the section of chain link in front of him.

The fence was electrified.

He backed off until he could turn and slog through the water to Takbar.

"Enough?" Takbar asked.

"More than enough. Let's get the hell out of here."

They moved back a good hundred yards and bore right. They increased their speed, swinging around the compound, watching the wall and watching for pursuit.

When they hit a footpath in the jungle, away from the paddies, they started to jog.

Twenty minutes later they made the clearing where the others waited. Anna was on Carter at once.

"Did you see him . . . is he really there?"

"No, we didn't see him, but he's there. He has to be." Carter grabbed her by the shoulders. "Aren't you worried about me?"

"Hell, no. You can take care of yourself."

"I'm hurt," he chuckled.

She struggled. Carter turned her to face him and pulled her to him. Her lips were slightly parted, as if she were waiting for a kiss.

She didn't get one.

Instead, his fingers bit into her flesh and his voice growled low in her ear. "Listen and listen good. I'm here to get those plans and put that compound out of business. My business comes first, and don't you forget it. If you want him, fine. But you get him *after* I'm done with him. Understand?"

She brought her hands up between them and with slow strength, little by little, she pushed and twisted her shoulders back and forth, trying to move away.

She couldn't. Carter's hands were gripping her like a vise.

"Understand?"

"Yes, damn you," she finally hissed.

"Good." He released her. "Sankjab?"

"Down here!"

Carter looked down. The little man had been standing right by their side the whole time. From the crooked grin on his face Carter knew that he was enjoying the caustic little exchange between him and Anna.

"The lady must want to see this Moultron man very much."

Carter threw Anna another look. The storm hadn't abated in her eyes.

"Yeah, she wants to see him real bad. Get a couple of lights over here."

Two men shielded flashlights as Carter cleared a spot on the ground with his hands. This done, he tensed his right forearm, and his stiletto, Hugo, jumped from its spring-loaded sheath into his palm.

"Interesting little item," Sankjab commented.

"Handy," Carter replied, and began laying out the interior of the compound in the dirt with the point of the stiletto.

Each man and Anna moved in close to the huddle and watched.

"The main house is here. The laboratory is the big one in the center. I think this is the kitchen and probably the mess hall here. This last hut is probably the sleeping quarters for the native help."

"How many men?" Sankjab asked.

"Probably two shifts of guards, sixteen in all. I imagine Moultron himself is alone in the house other than for a servant or two. He wouldn't stoop to share with the masses."

"Servants?"

"Couldn't tell," Carter replied. "I saw only a couple of women, here, by the cook shack. With the amount of guards and their need for privacy, I'd say no more than five, maybe six."

"Okay, big man," Sankjab said, rubbing his palms together, "how do we take it?"

"We cut through the fence, one man here on the north perimeter, one man here, on the south. You, Sankjab, and a third man cut through about here, on the corner. When you are through, make your way toward the front gate. There's a small hut there on stilts. You can hide under it until it's time to make war."

"I no go in?" Takbar exclaimed.

"Oh, yeah," Carter replied, moving the point of the stiletto to the rear of the compound behind the big house. "You, with the Bren, Anna, and I go in here."

Takbar dropped into a squat with his eyes narrowed.

"You no speak of fence yet."

"What about the fence?" Sankjab asked.

"It's electrified, but I can take care of that. Takbar, can you swing back to that last village we passed and get me a rice hook?"

The man nodded.

"Also, we'll need to strip one full coil of detonating wire and rewire the bare strands by hand."

Sankjab looked puzzled for a moment, and then he smiled. "You're going to short it."

"That's right. The insulation is rotted away in a dozen places on every wire. I doubt if they have an emergency battery generator for a backup. They'll probably have to restart the diesel generator. That should take at least five minutes, hopefully more. By the time they get the lights back on, we should be through the fence and in place."

"And the dogs?" Takbar asked.

"We saw only one, and he was more pet than watchdog. If there are others, I think they'll be the same. They'll bark and raise hell in the confusion of the darkness and everyone running around, but they'll quiet down when order is restored."

Sankjab canvassed his men to make sure they understood everything up to that point. When he was satisfied, he turned back to Carter.

"How do we go when they get the lights back on?"

"We don't," Carter said, "at least not right away. I'm going into the house and try to take Moultron. If I get him first, we might not have to go to war. If I read him right, his own skin is the most important thing to him. If it means saving it, he'll call off his dogs."

The flame on the little man's cigar glowed bright red as he sucked hard on it and swung his head from side to side. "No way, I think. These are Dr. Sung's people. They know only fight when they are cornered. My thinking is they will fight first and listen to this Moultron man later."

"Maybe so," Carter agreed, "but it's a good risk, if we can take them quietly. Takbar, you can set up the Bren here, under the front veranda of the house. From there you can spray that entire side of the compound."

The big man nodded.

"And if you have trouble with Moultron," Sankjab asked, "what is the signal for us to go?"

"No precise signal," Carter replied. "If something blows, it blows, and we all start shooting. Everything clear?"

Heads nodded all around. Takbar moved off into the darkness, and the others found their own space to prepare themselves and their weapons.

Anna and Carter were left alone.

"You're trusting me to go in with you?" she asked.

"Yeah, I am. My guess is Moultron knows about you. He's probably more afraid of you than he is of me."

She chuckled. "And you called *me* hard. You will use me to get him to do as you say."

"That's right, and you remember it. I want to do two things . . . get the plans for the device, and blow up that laboratory."

"And when that's done, I get Moultron?"

"You get Moultron," Carter said, and moved away to be by himself.

He didn't want to look at the bloodlust in her eyes.

TWELVE

It was the dull part of the nighttime hours, around four in the morning. It was that time after midnight and just before dawn when boredom sets in and the sharp edge of alertness is dulled.

Quiet had descended on the compound, a silence with tenseness in it. Everything was about the same as it had been on the previous jaunt. The fires in the cook shack had been banked. There were a few lights on the first level of the main house, but they were dim. Ditto with the longhouse, showing one spot of ruddy lamplight through its single door.

Carter paused beyond the cleared space outside the fence and studied the big structure that he was sure housed the testing facility that would soon be used for Moultron's form of international blackmail.

It was built of massive timbers, with walls of slat-work. Its length, as he had already estimated, was better than a hundred yards. It was all of two hundred feet wide, supported on pilings that lifted it higher than a tall man could reach. A platform ran all the way around, with ladders placed at twenty- to twenty-five-foot intervals.

It was this platform that intrigued Carter. It was in total darkness. If he could get on it unobserved, he could plant plastique with transmitter-controlled detonators in strategic spots before going into the house to face Moultron.

If this could be done successfully, no matter how the outcome of his face-off with the traitor, he could be sure of blowing the laboratory and achieving half his purpose.

Anna appeared at his side, her dark-smudged face close to his. "What is it . . . something wrong?"

"No, just a thought," he replied. "But I think my first one is my best one."

He shifted his attention to his right and the big, main house. It was a seemingly haphazard assortment of additions to a central, two-story portion, all with sway-back roofs and gables surmounted by Oriental-style round spires. It was built on piles, but it was not as high as the longhouse containing the laboratory.

A veranda ran along the front. The veranda was strewn with old straw sitting pads, tables, screens, and mats. There were six or seven doors leading from the veranda to various rooms of the house. All the doors were draped with filthy brindle and striped cotton. The drapes waved in the slight breeze that passed through the house. No one was in sight.

Moultron had the best of the compound, Carter thought, but even he had been forced into roughing it.

Carter lay, watching the two guards exchange words, turn, and start back on their long walk to meet two other guards. When they were a safe distance away, he started forward.

"Stay down," he hissed, "and be ready with the cutters. Remember, just the lowest strands so we can reset them."

There were two guttural agreements from Takbar and Anna, and Carter was at the fence.

Carefully, he uncoiled the peeled detonator wire. It had been meticulously rewound by hand and nipped at both ends. Takbar had heated and bent a rice knife until it had formed a heavy hook, which Carter had attached to one end of the wire.

He strung the bare wire out, playing out enough to reach the electric line that ran above the compound fence, supplying power to the post lights and, in turn, to the fence itself.

When this was done to his satisfaction, he spent a minute or two more studying the line itself. It was dark with only a reflected glow from the lights, but he could tell by the slight glow where the insulation had rotted away.

He heard a clicking sound behind him, a warning from Takbar.

The guard to his right had broken his rhythm and was already returning. Carter flattened himself to the ground, practically holding his breath with his face straight down, and waited.

He focused his full concentration on sound. The steady tread of one and then the other guard's bush boots on the soft ground. Then the sound stopped, not more than twenty feet directly in front of him.

Carter's hand tensed on the silenced Luger he had placed in a hip holster earlier.

The wait seemed forever. A match flared. He could hear the exhalation of one of the guards blowing out the first deep drag from a cigarette.

Some words were exchanged in Chinese, and then he heard again the steady tread of the boots.

He accustomed himself to the pacing rhythm of the guards, then, waiting for his best chance, he rose and spun the wire heavily weighted by the makeshift hook.

He let the arc grow wider and wider, and then tossed it high and far.

He held his breath as it sailed toward the night sky, and then exhaled with relief as it dropped over the line and he saw the hook gently swinging.

Its swinging caused a jiggling of the light.

He hadn't counted on that, so he quickly backed off, drawing the wire taut. In no time the hook came up to catch solidly on the wire. As he moved backward, he dragged the hook along the wire with a series of jerks, hunting for one of the bare spots.

Suddenly, sparks crackled.

"Get ready!" he hissed into the darkness behind him, and let the bare wire fall forward.

It hit the electrified chain link with an immediate hissing sound.

There was a brief flash of white, and the wires shorted. Instantly, the entire compound was thrown into darkness, with the exception of a few lanterns in the servants' barracks and a dim light in the cook shack.

"Now!" Carter barked. "Quickly."

In an instant, Anna and Takbar were by his side. All three of them began clipping with wire cutters.

"Remember," Carter whispered, "not too high."

In no time they had cut a swath two feet high and three feet across. The two men had barely bent it up before Anna was wriggling through. Carter and then Takbar followed.

As the big Malay bent the fence down and secured it as much as he could, Carter freed the hook with a series of jerks. In seconds the hook fell to the ground. Carter gathered hook and wire, coiled them, and flung them as hard as he could over the fence into the darkness.

"Hurry! This way!"

The three of them, in single file and crouched low, moved through the deep shadows toward the house. All around the end of the longhouse. A spotlight on its roof was weaving from side to side, its beam floating along the side of the fence to locate the trouble.

Above them they heard a window being thrown open and a husky voice calling out in English.

"What is it? What the hell is all the noise about?"

A guard ran past, so close they could have reached out with a gun barrel and touched him. He stopped not ten feet in front of them.

"Something shorted wire. It blew breaker." The words were in broken English.

"Goddamned bats."

"Maybe snake," cackled the Chinese, padding away.

"Him!" Anna tensed.

Carter clutched her shoulder. He had known who it was as well. *Moultron*.

At least Carter now knew the man's location.

A set of headlights came on, and a truck came roaring around the end of the longhouse. A spotlight on its roof was weaving from side to side, its beam floating along the side of the fence to locate the trouble.

A Chinese on the truck and another on the ground shouted to one another. The one on the ground said that a wire had burned off, and the one in the truck dug around in a box of gear, tossing out several items, one of which was a set of electrician's climbing irons. His companion put on the irons and mounted the pole.

"They won't be more than ten minutes repairing that wire and getting the lights back on," Carter whispered to Takbar. "Get set up!"

Takbar moved further back into the darkness, and Carter could hear the sounds of the Bren being set up on its tripod. He turned to Anna.

"You ready?"

"I've been ready for a long time," she murmured coldly.

"Okay, stay close and cover my ass."

He rolled from beneath the veranda, with her close behind him. In single file they ran to the rear and mounted some steps.

It was fairly quiet now that they had found the source of the problem. Besides the occasional bark of a dog and voices from the area of the repair truck, everything was the same as it had been when they arrived.

They reached the rear veranda, and Carter stopped to get his bearings. Barely by sight, more by smell, he found the kitchen and a screened, roofed-over passage leading into the house.

"There is light from that room down the hall," Anna whispered, gesturing beyond the kitchen area.

"I see it," Carter said, moving ahead.

The door to the kitchen opened at his touch. The pilot light of a propane stove, hissing softly, gave off a faint bluish light. It guided them around tables and counters, through warm spice smells to the passageway.

They stopped, listened. No sound.

They went on slowly, groping their way, using their hands against the wall, moving toward the light that flickered through a partially opened door.

When they reached it, Carter dropped to his knees and pulled Anna down beside him. Both of them leaned forward and peered through the crack.

The room was dark save for the ruddy glow of a tiny charcoal stove. A man sat cross-legged on a piece of straw matting—a middle-sized, middle-aged man, very ſim, probably of mixed Chinese and Malay blood. He was dressed in the Chinese-Malay manner, too, in a turban of the kapala type, in a robe of black, in loose trousers also of a dark hue. On his feet were simple sandals. He was holding a heavy copper pan in which he had brewed tea from water heated over the charcoal. The charcoal was not the purest carbon and its smoke filled the air.

Carter mouthed, "Servant," and Anna nodded.

He was about to push the door open, when another directly behind the squatting man opened. A young girl entered and seated herself across from the man in the identical position.

She was beautiful, with an almost English cast of features, but very dark-eyed and dark-skinned. She, too, was dressed in trousers, black cotton, held by a drawstring pulled tight above her small, round abdomen. But instead of the loose blouse of the men, she wore a vest of stiff brocade without fastenings in the front, open and revealing her breasts.

The girl spoke in Malay. The man grimaced and nodded as he began to pour the tea.

Carter put his lips to Anna's ear. "What did she say?"

Anna did the same, leaning close. "She said she has serviced the pig for the night and he is already snoring."

"So much for help these days. Let's go!"

Carter drew the silenced Luger and they moved into the room, one to the right, one to the left.

The girl didn't even bother to lift her eyes. The old man's face didn't change expression.

"Tell them we want them to answer a few questions. Tell them if they answer truthfully and make no noise, they won't be harmed."

Anna relayed Carter's words in Malay. The old man

merely shrugged and sipped his tea.

"How many other servants in the house?"

Anna spoke, and relayed the man's answer. "One, a boy, the girl's brother."

"Where is he and which room is Moultron's?"

Again the question, answer, and translation. "The boy sleeps upstairs on a mat near the white man's room, should he want anything in the night. It is the large bedroom in the front. The stairs are in the rear, through the main downstairs rooms."

"Good. Tell him that we're sorry but we will have to tie them up and gag them."

Anna spoke. Again the man only shrugged. The young girl looked up at Carter, at the gun in his hand, and pointed at a small ebony chest in the corner.

She spoke, and Anna translated. "She says there is twine in there that they use for the washing, to dry it."

"I figured they would be cooperative," Carter growled. "Get it. And save some for the boy upstairs."

It took less than five minutes to securely bind the two of them. As Anna set the gag over the girl's mouth, they exchanged several words.

"What does she want?" Carter asked.

"Nothing."

"Bullshit. What did she say?"

"She asked me if we were going to kill the pig."

"And?"

"I told her that we were," Anna said. "As slowly as possible."

Again they were in the hall, groping with their hands. The wall was smoothly plastered rather than the usual breathing wall of slotted bamboo.

They found a door and a change in the hall's direction. The door opened with a creak, and they stepped into the main room of the house. They could see now by the faint moonlight coming through two front windows.

The room was empty of furniture and it had the smell of abandonment, the peculiar, musty odor that fills the best of houses anywhere after a few months without regular occupancy.

"There, a door," Anna whispered.

Carter nodded. He was about to move, when bright light flooded through the windows and a cheer came up from the guards.

"Everything's luck now," Carter whispered, and headed for the door in a duck walk.

Beyond it was another hall leading to a flight of stairs. They were nearly to the stairs when they could hear someone moving, the slight creak of footsteps descending.

The steps came closer, and then they saw him, the servant boy, in shorts and a white jacket. He was carrying a tray with a bottle and a glass.

He hit the bottom step and moved toward them. He came straight down the hall without looking up and would have passed them except that Carter moved out from the wall and blocked his way.

Just as the boy saw him, Carter seized him. He turned him quickly and caught his neck in the bend of his left arm. He saved the glass and bottle from falling by holding them against the boy's chest with his other arm.

"Grab them!" Carter hissed.

Anna did, avoiding any clatter, and the boy started to struggle.

He was only about fifteen, but he was built solidly and put up a struggle that occupied all of Carter's weight and strength for several seconds.

But the arm soon cut off his wind and he gave up,

going limp in Carter's grasp.

"Anna!" Carter said, easing him to the floor and putting a knee in his gut.

"Do not cry out," she said in Malay. "We will not hurt you. Where is the white man?"

"Upstairs, the front room. He sends me for fresh water."

"Is he alone?"

"Yes."

Anna relayed the information.

"Tie his feet with the cord."

As she did, the Killmaster tore his jacket into strips and bound his wrists. With the last two pieces he gagged him and rolled him against the wall.

As they headed back for the stairs, Carter accidentally kicked the glass that Anna had set on the floor. It clanked and went rolling away.

Carter cursed. They both froze and listened. He thought he heard a step in the hall above them, but after a full minute there was nothing.

They went up the stairs, taking them slowly until they hit the upper landing. Dimly he could see a curtained window at the end of a long hall, and right beside it an open door.

Halfway down the hall he paused. He had the feeling that someone was close to him. It was something he could feel rather than see.

Then he actually saw movement, across the hall on Anna's side. There was a dull thud and a cry of pain from Anna. Carter stepped forward, and her limp form was thrust against him. He staggered, off-balance, and saw the bulk of a man coming at him, faintly silhouetted in the light from the window.

It had to be Moultron.

Carter pushed Anna to the side and swung the barrel of the Thompson upward.

Its muzzle caught the man a ripping blow in the vicinity of his gut. With the gun high, Carter came down with it, trying to smash the man's skull. But Moultron was moving forward and took the blow half force. He went to his knees, trying to wrap his arms around Carter's legs, and Carter kicked him away and tramped his head on the floor.

It was all without the aid of sight. He tried to get clear of Moultron's fallen body. He had no feeling that anyone was in front of him; all he knew was that something had hit him, and now he was down, trying to get up from the floor.

He got to one knee, gathered his strength, and lunged to his feet. He collided with someone. He knew it was Moultron. They reeled in each other's grasp. Moultron outweighed him, but Carter was taller with an advantage in reach.

He burst free. Swinging, he tried to keep the man away where his reach would help him. He tried to punch until he recovered from the blow that had put him on the floor. A left landed, and he brought up the right, hoping blindly for the jaw. It struck and paralyzed his arm with pain. Moultron had taken it on the top of the head.

With head down, Moultron charged. He carried Carter back. The wall stopped him. He tried to slip aside, but Moultron had him with a half nelson and a stranglehold.

Carter drove both knees upward to Moultron's groin. Grunting, Moultron took them and bore down harder, pinning Carter's throat to the wall with his elbow, holding him with the nelson.

The air was gone from Carter's lungs. He fought through black dizziness, through blackness turned to dancing light and exploding meteors in his eyeballs. He could feel the gathering of Moultron's muscles for the final application of pressure that would crush the bone and cartilage of his throat, and parrying it, he managed to twist his head and at the same instant he let his knees collapse.

Moultron tried to smash him harder against the wall, but Carter was down, doubled over in the right angle of floor and wall. He twisted, drew himself into a ball, and drove out with both feet. Moultron was down over him.

Ordinarily he might have seized that momentary advantage, but he lacked strength; his lungs were still screaming for air. He rolled, and he got free.

He had dropped the Thompson, but he had no idea where. He felt for it on the floor. He got up and took a step and his toe hit it, sending it clattering away across the floor. He staggered after it, tripped, and fell. He crawled, hunting it. He tried to get up and collided hard with the wall, knocking himself down again. And there was the gun making a hard bar beneath him.

He got hold of it and tried to draw it from under his body, but its forward sight caught and his own weight was holding it down. He engaged in a mad, blind wrestle with the gun before he got his wits about him.

He stood and lifted the Thompson. He turned in the direction he saw movement, and flipped the safety off.

"You're obviously not armed, Moultron. I am. This is a Thompson. You move or cry out and I'll spray this whole goddamned hall. You hear?"

Silence.

"I said, you hear, you bastard?"

"*Ja, Ja,* I hear."

"Good. Anna!"

"Over here."

"You all right?"

"I'll live."

"Snap on your flash."

She did, waving it until it landed on Moultron's big body. He had a deep gash up his middle that was bleeding through his undershirt. His only other clothing was a pair of baggy boxer shorts.

Carter took a quick look at Anna. One eye was already going black, and there was a bluish cast to the left side of her face. Other than that she still looked mean as hell.

Moultron was swiveling his head from side to side, trying to get past the beam of light to get a better look at them.

"What do you want . . . who are you?"

Anna stepped forward, drew back, and landed a solid right in the middle of Moultron's gut.

He whooshed air and sat down with her directly over him.

"I'm your judge, jury, and executioner, you son of a bitch."

THIRTEEN

He was big, two-forty at least, and mostly muscle despite his age. Since the initial battle in the hall he had calmed, and now seemed unperturbed about their presence or the nasty gash in his belly.

They had moved him back into the bedroom at the point of their guns. Carter had tightly closed the heavy curtains over the window and lit a single, low-watt bulb suspended from one of the ceiling beams.

Now Moultron sat in a high-backed rattan chair, shifting his eyes from Carter to Anna and back again. His wide face was calm, almost sporting a smile.

"You are Carter."

"I am."

"You are a very worthy opponent, Carter. Dr. Sung sincerely believes that you are still in Hong Kong."

Carter smiled. "With the hell my friends are giving Dr. Sung's organization all over Sotheast Asia, Moultron, I doubt that he'll worry too much about your little deal when I blow it all to hell."

Moultron seemed to relish the Killmaster's words. He laughed. It was a satisfied laugh, deep in his thick throat. He sat forward a trifle, the chair seat too low for a man of his size, his legs bent, the shorts drawn tautly over his thick thighs. His belly, big without being fat, thrust forward between his knees, and his huge shoulders rounded as he prepared to speak.

"You underestimate Dr. Sung for several reasons. What you have done is a taint upon his honor, his leadership. The Chinese hate to lose face. He will have to kill you for that alone. Also, the good doctor relishes the huge commission my efforts will provide him. You would do better for yourself and those you represent to let my little auction take place. Perhaps that would mollify him."

Carter matched the other man's calm smile and lit a cigarette. "Dr. Sung can go to hell. I'm here for two things, Moultron: the master plan to your device, and to blow this compound to hell."

"You think you can do that?" Moultron chortled. "There are twenty of Dr. Sung's best out there."

"That's covered."

"Perhaps," Moultron said, letting his gaze shift to Anna. "You are very beautiful, as she was, before she grew old and tired."

Anna tensed, and her knuckles on the Thompson turned white.

"Easy," Carter murmured, "he's just trying to provoke you. Where are the plans, Moultron?"

"In my head."

"Not according to Pletov. They are written down and already sealed, to be delivered along with the model of the device to go to the highest bidder."

The hard eyes moved back to Carter. "What else did that fool tell you?"

"That the device works. That he has copies of your plans, and that when I have yours he will sell us his at a much lower price."

Moultron's bushy eyebrows arched sharply. "And you believe him?"

"For the time being. I don't have much time, Moultron. I want the plans, and I want you to order Dr.

Sung's guards to throw down their arms."

Again he laughed. "I was wrong, Carter. You are as big a fool as this one is a whore."

The tight string of Anna's anger snapped. She cast aside the Thompson and drew the bush knife from her belt. Before Carter could stop her, she was behind Moultron. She gripped his thick head of graying hair and savagely yanked his head back. At the same time, she drew blood from his neck with the point of the knife.

"Tell him, you pig!" she hissed. "Tell him what he wants to know so we can get this over with!"

"You think you have me, don't you?" Moultron growled.

"I have you, pig, by the hair, the throat. I could kill you this instant. Or I could take out your eyeballs with a flick of this knife and then run bamboo through your inner ears. I can chop off your fingers, one by one, and when I am finished you'll even forget your name. You'll know only pain. After that, I wouldn't even have to kill you. You would do it for me, to stop the pain."

Carter held his ground. It was a frightening tableau. All the years of hatred that had built up in Anna came out at that instant. Carter could see it, practically smell it. And he could see that Moultron also saw it. His guess that Moultron would fear Anna more than himself was true.

Or so he thought.

Beads of sweat broke out on Moultron's face and neck. There was a slight tremor in his body.

"I'll tell you when—"

"Now!" Anna hissed.

"The knife . . . take the knife away first."

Slowly she pulled the knife a few inches from his throat.

Moultron moved with amazing speed for his size. His elbow came back with a jolting thud into Anna's pelvis. In a fraction of a second he sprang from the chair and was on her.

Before Carter could draw the silenced Lugar, Moultron had her by the front of the blouse. He lifted her from her feet like a feather, twisted her around, and dragged her close to his own body. She became a shield against Carter's gun while he tore the knife from her hand.

Anna had been jerked senseless for a moment, her neck almost out of joint. Then she began to fight with the blind fury of a captured animal. She flapped her arms, trying to kick, bite, do anything to writhe free. But Moultron had her.

"Shoot, Carter," the man said, laughing.

He held her and swung her from side to side, keeping her off-balance as he backed toward the door. The constant movement gave Carter no chance to use the gun.

When Anna stopped kicking, Moultron used the pause to press the needle-sharp point against her throat. Moultron kept moving toward the door, forcing Anna's head further back.

She had no thought of struggle now. She was rigid. The muscles and tendons stood out on her neck, her eyes were bulging, she breathed with difficulty, and it was the loudest sound in the room.

"Put the gun down, Carter," Moultron hissed.

It had all happened so quickly. Carter had the Lugar aimed but dared not shoot. Each time he maneuvered for a clear shot, Moultron swung the helpless woman between them.

Now he was in the doorway, and suddenly Anna came to life.

"Shoot!" she cried. "Shoot, Nick, kill us both!"

"Yes, Carter," Moultron said, "shoot. Kill us both, or I'll skewer her from ear—"

Suddenly his words turned into a gagging gasp. The knife dropped from his hand and Anna slithered to the floor. Moultron staggered a step or two back into the room, and turned.

There, standing in the doorway, her eyes wide, a grim smile on her face, was the young girl they had left tied up below.

And protruding from the center of Moultron's back was the hilt of a rice knife.

Carter raised the Luger, but before he could fire, Moultron let out with a guttural roar. He grasped the young girl by the shoulders, turned, and lifted her high above his head. He literally flung her at the Killmaster.

Carter got off one shot around the girl's body, but it went wild into the doorjamb.

He could hear pounding feet down the stairs, and a second later the slam of one of the doors.

There was little doubt of it now. His initial plan was down the drain. The alternate was to kill Moultron, blow the compound to hell, and hope that the plans went up with it if he couldn't find them.

He rushed to the window and ripped off the drapes. With the barrel of the Thompson he smashed out the glass.

Moultron was running across the open part of the compound, shouting like hell, heading for the laboratory.

Ten to one, Carter thought, *that's where the plans will be!*

He tried to sight in and fire off a whole magazine at the running figure. Moultron's wound was obviously far from lethal. Even with the knife still protruding from his back, he zigzagged enough to avoid being hit.

Between Moultron's shouting and the chatter of the Thompson, all hell broke loose. Men came running from everywhere and gunfire erupted from all parts of the compound.

Carter was fairly sure that, because of the element of surprise, Sankjab's men could hold their own.

His point was soon proved.

Three guards came racing around the side of the long-house directly toward the main house. They had their guns at the ready, but because they couldn't see their enemy they weren't firing.

Their mistake.

From directly below Carter's window, the big Bren began to bark. Takbar took all three of them with his first burst.

Two more came from the other side. Carter had already jacked a new clip into the Thompson. He got the first one, Takbar the second, making their bodies dance like puppets on a string before falling lifeless to the ground.

"Takbar!" Carter yelled.

"Here!"

"Get out—form up with the others! I'm going to blow the house!"

There was no verbal answer. Instead, Carter could follow the man as he fired his own cover, sprinting sideways down the fence line.

Carter returned to Anna, who sat, somewhat stunned, on the floor. He found her Thompson and shoved it into her hands.

"C'mon, let's get the hell out of here."

"He got away. The bastard got away!"

Gently but firmly he slapped her face. "But not for long. Now move!"

Before leaving the room, Carter scanned it for the

young servant girl. She was gone. He guessed that she would probably have freed the old man and her brother as well.

He was right. The boy was not at the bottom of the stairs.

Carter paused long enough to plant a wad of plastique, set a detonator for two minutes, and jam it into the mass.

"C'mon!"

With Anna close behind him, Carter led the way back through the dark house toward the rear. As they ran, he readied another plastique bomb, which he left in the kitchen.

He was about to open the door to the veranda, when he heard the sound of boots and backed off.

Suddenly the door opened . . . on nothing. But from beyond it Carter caught the odor of human sweat and tobacco.

Then he was there, a guard moving through the doorway. Carter laid the barrel of the Thompson across his skull and shot him as he fell.

The man went out with a scream. He hit the floor on elbows and knees, a thud that shook the house. A second man shouted in alarm. Someone was running. Guards seemed to be everywhere beyond the veranda. Carter fired a burst, which was quickly returned.

The time on the detonators was ticking off in his head.

"This way!"

They ran toward the north side of the house down a long, dark hall. Suddenly the light came on and a man stepped from a side room.

Before Carter could fire, Anna took him with a burst. It lifted him from the floor and flattened him against the door.

"Glad to see you're back to being your old self," Carter joked.

She didn't answer.

Carter got the body away from the door. It was barred, whether on the inside or outside he couldn't take time to find out.

He drew back and hit the door shoulder first, smashing it free of its hinges.

They were on the veranda.

Outside everything was chaos, with running, shouting men and the constant chatter of gunfire. One of the huts was burning, turning that section of the compound into daylight.

Carter couldn't be sure, but from a quick eyeball count of fallen bodies he guessed that Sankjab's men were winning the battle so far.

"Over the side!" Carter yelled, dropping from the veranda and reaching back to help Anna.

A guard ran past without even looking at them. Carter charted a course across the man's back with the Thompson, nearly splitting him in half. Men were on the move all across the compound, leaderless, without order.

That was good.

A few of them carried torches, making themselves perfect targets in the blistering crossfire from Sankjab's men. Dawn was a glow that silhouetted the tops of the huts and buildings but left the ground still in darkness.

"Where?" Anna panted as they ran.

"The laboratory building," Carter replied. "He's probably after the plans."

They were halfway there when the world exploded behind them, sending both of them sprawling to the ground. One look told Carter the plastique had done its job. Two walls were blown clear away from the main house and the whole thing was one big pyre.

"You all right?"

"Yes," Anna nodded, already on her feet.

They climbed one of the ladders to the elevated walkway. Carter was ready with a fresh clip in the Thompson to cut down anyone they encountered.

Just in case, he put a burst through the door before they entered.

The inside was about what he had figured. There was a huge tank with a flattened map of the entire world stretched taut just above the water's dark surface. Observation catwalks ran back and forth above the tank, and one whole wall was banked with television monitors.

Tiny models of submarines—probably radio-controlled—were dotted around the map.

It was the perfect setup for Moultron to prove his device.

There was a large, glassed-in box at the far end of the building. It was like a press box far above the field in a football stadium. He wasn't sure, but Carter thought he saw movement behind the glass as they started to move around the tank.

It was confirmed when one of the glass panels flew open and the ugly snout of an assault rifle poked through.

Carter went to the deck and took Anna with him just in time, as slugs peppered the air above their heads.

"This way, the other side!" he barked.

They ran, only to be followed by the glare of a spotlight and more gunfire. The slugs tore up the floor past them, away from them, and back again.

The wall of the tank was in front of them. Carter flung the woman so that she fell, rolling like a supple ball into its cover, and he followed headfirst.

They were in a sort of gutter or trough that ran all the way around the huge tank.

"Go, go!" he yelled, keeping her moving ahead of him while the bullets ricocheted off the steel above them.

The tank ended. Carter stopped, holding Anna by one ankle to keep her from going too far.

Suddenly everything was quiet. Carter raised his head to look around.

He was about to pop the searchlight with the Thompson, when the entire glass enclosure far above erupted. Flame and glass shot in every direction.

Carter dug his face into the wood flooring and rolled to cover Anna's body with his. The sound was deafening and kept rolling in waves like thunder.

Carter could feel the glass shards falling across their backs and the rumbling aftershock of the explosion ripple through the floor.

He chanced a quick look when the initial, deafening roar had died down to just the sound of crackling flames.

"What is it?" Anna asked. "What happened?"

"He blew it," Carter hissed. "That was probably the control area where he had the device and the control computers set up. He blew it to hell."

Her voice came back in a low monotone. "Where is he?"

"Ten to one he wasn't in there when it went."

He looked around. They were still in the rounded gutter affair. He was about to stand, when two simultaneous explosions ripped out the sides of the tank itself. One was on the other side, and the other was on their side about seventy feet behind them.

"Oh, my God, the water!" he breathed. "On your feet, hurry!"

Water was pouring into the gutter where they stood at a thousand gallons per second from the ruptures in the tank. It was coming at them from the rear, and soon it would round the corner coming from the other side to sandwich them in the middle.

"That ladder! Move!"

He yanked her along behind him, both of them running for the steel-runged ladder about fifty feet away. The rush of water was deafening in its surge as they reached the ladder. Carter grasped Anna by the hips and practically threw her up the first few rungs. She caught and moved as if the hounds of hell were after her, with Carter scrambling close behind.

She rolled over the top of the ladder to the narrow walkway just as the torrents of water merged. Carter was still on the ladder, half his body from the waist down still in the gutter.

The pressure was powerful, like a vise on his hips and legs. He locked his arms around the ladder and held on. It was all he could do.

Above him he could see Anna's white face and her arm reaching out to help him.

"No!" he cried. "Stay back—it's too powerful! It will suck—"

He couldn't get the rest of the words out. The water had surged to its fullest. It pushed against his ribs, threatening to crush him like an eggshell.

Then, just as quickly, it ebbed, trying to suck him back into the gutter. The pull was incredible, and he could feel his arms beginning to give way.

Then he heard voices. He looked up. Takbar and a second man had Sankjab by the ankles. The little man's head was right by his, and Carter could feel a rope being slipped under his armpits.

"Hang on!" Sankjab hissed in his ear, "hang on, only a few seconds!"

Somewhere in the distance there was the scream and shriek of steel shredding. Carter didn't have to look to know that the water pressure was collapsing the tank. In no time it would hit the pilings and the whole building would collapse.

Then Sankjab was gone and Carter could feel the pressure of the water on his body receding as he was pulled free.

Suddenly he was stretched out on the platform, spouting like a beached whale.

"The pilings!" Sankjab shouted. "They are going to go! Hurry, carry him!"

Carter felt himself heaved up on someone's shoulder and he passed out.

FOURTEEN

He was out only a few minutes and came to stretched flat on the ground in the middle of the compound. Anna lay nearby, gasping to get air into her lungs. Sankjab was squatting over him, and the other men stood nearby with their guns up, still ready even though the battle was clearly over.

Carter rolled his eyes around the compound and saw near total devastation. The laboratory building was completely collapsed. The main house was only a smoldering cinder, as were the barracks buildings.

"How did we do?" the Killmaster groaned, rising to a sitting position.

"Nineteen of theirs dead, one wounded and dying."

"The servants?"

"Two accounted for, the rest scattered. I imagine they got out when it first started."

"Ours?"

"One dead," the little man said. "Moultron ambushed him when he was getting away. My man went after him, and . . ." He shook his head slowly.

"Then Moultron got away?"

Sankjab shrugged. "Depends. He was staggering and bleeding like a stuck pig. He can't be going too far like that, and he's only got a twenty-minute head start."

Before Carter could reply, Anna was on her feet. "Which way?"

Her words said it all. In five minutes they were all assembled and moving out.

There was no need for concealment now, just speed. With Takbar doing the tracking, they stayed on open footpaths, moving swiftly. Twice, without pausing, the big Malay pointed to spots of blood on the ground.

Moultron was badly wounded. Carter knew it was only a matter of time.

They were about a mile out when they realized he was taking the same trails back toward the ocean that they had taken to come in.

"The bridge," Carter said.

Takbar nodded, grim-faced. "We must reach it before he crosses. If he gets across and cuts or destroys it, it will be impossible to catch him. It would take a whole day to get around the head of the gorge."

With full dawn came the rain that had been threatening. Clouds hid the mountains, and, in the form of a very wet fog, descended around the path they followed.

It made the going rougher, but they knew it would also be rougher for their prey.

About an hour later, a state of near exhaustion forced Carter to call a halt. Despite the rain, it was hot. The humidity was stifling. Carter moved to where Takbar squatted, still on the trail.

"Could we have passed him in the fog?"

"It's possible but not likely. He doesn't run like a fox, but like a wounded ox, straight in the line his brain tells him is safe."

They dared not rest long. In five minutes they were up and going again, trying to reach the fragile, swaying bridge over the deep gorge and the river before Moultron.

They sighted the second, small village they had

passed, and Takbar jogged off the trail to speak to an old man bent over digging rice sprouts.

He was back in seconds. "He is no more than five minutes in front of us."

They went on more carefully, through thorn and tree clumps, watching for ambush. Ahead somewhere in the mist was a great rift in the earth's crust. Carter remembered coming across the bridge when it was dry . . . the sway, and the fact that only two could cross at a time . . .

They emerged from the undergrowth. A mist rising from the river merged with the mist of the rain. The bridge hung perfectly still without a tremble, its ropes dark from the soaking fog, the wooden slats of the footway shiny with moisture.

"There!" Takbar said, pointing.

Carter strained his eyes. Slowly they focused. Moultron was on the slats, on his belly, crawling steadily forward, pulling himself along slat by slat. Around his neck, attached by a leather strap, was a briefcase. He had somehow pulled the knife from his back, but the damage it had done was easily spotted.

Takbar fingered the Bren. "It would be an easy shot from here."

"No," Carter said softly. "I want that briefcase."

"You're a fool!" Anna cried.

"Aren't we all, at times?"

"Then I'm going out there with you."

"Has it eaten you up so bad?"

"Yes," she hissed, and headed for the bridge.

Carter caught her and moved ahead. "Then stay ten paces or so behind me. It will steady the sway."

She nodded, and Carter took the first few tentative steps. Ahead of them, Moultron felt the pressure and turned, his eyes wild with pain.

When he saw them he pulled himself to his feet and tried moving faster. Suddenly he paused and turned, lifting his arm.

Too late, Carter saw the Mauser in the other man's hand and heard it roar. The bullet struck the footway, leaving one of the slats broken, its fragments dangling.

Carter kept on, hunched forward. He skidded and almost fell. A second bullet whipped close by and he lay on his stomach, fearing to rise, clinging with both arms wrapped around the footway.

Then the bridge started swaying crazily. Carter looked back. Anna was on her knees, her hands on the ropes, jerking them and rolling her body from side to side.

He started to curse her, when Moultron did it for him. The man was thrown from his feet. He grappled wildly for a handhold, and in so doing dropped the Mauser. It sailed out and down, disappearing in the rising mist.

Carter lurched to his feet and started forward with a bent-over, swaying stride.

From a leather sheath at his belt Moultron drew a machete. He stood, feet wide, one hand on the ropes, awaiting Carter's charge. He was at once both a tragic and a comic figure. He was blood from his neck to his hips and still dressed in the ridiculous boxer shorts. His undershirt was in tatters, and through it, where there was no blood, his skin gleamed a soft pink.

Carter would have laughed if it hadn't been for the swinging machete.

"Toss it in, Moultron! It's all over! Just give me the briefcase!"

"Go to hell, Carter! Go to hell!"

To the Killmaster's surprise, Moultron started advancing steadily toward him in a fighting crouch.

Then he saw it. It was in the face and eyes. The face had a loose, flabby expression and the eyes were vacant, mad.

Moultron had gone over. He didn't care now if he lived or died. All he had left was his basic savagery.

Carter stopped and Moultron kept coming. He neither increased nor diminished his speed until he had covered the last few steps between them. He came as if he expected to trample Carter underfoot.

Making the last stride, he swung the machete in a horizontal arc, putting all the power of his massive body into it.

Had it struck it might well have cut Carter in half, for the knife was razor sharp with a weight of four or five pounds. But Carter fell backward, landing unsteadily on the narrow, slatted walk. There he felt the power of the knife pass over him. Then he rose, doubled over, coming forward, his fist up, trying to catch the big man at an unbalanced moment.

Moultron proved too quick.

Instinctively, realizing that his momentum would not let him turn back, he powered on, letting go of the rope and seizing Carter's wrist. At the same time, he fell forward across the Killmaster, trying to use his weight to force the point of the machete down.

But Carter was steeled against the man's weight and his weakened condition. They fought, lying full length on the narrow footway, each holding the arms of the other.

For the briefest of seconds, Carter freed his right arm. Instantly, Hugo leaped into his palm.

Moultron cursed at the evening of the odds, and managed to grip Carter's wrist again. The renewed anger seemed to pump new adrenaline into his weakened body.

They were locked without advantage. That lasted ten or twelve seconds. Then Moultron's position and superior weight began to assert itself. Slowly, with the application of terrific strength, he was able to turn Carter's stiletto a degree, and another, and another. The position of his own knife remained the same, pointed downward at Carter's abdomen. The advantage was very slow, but very certain.

Moultron was wheezing through his nose. He was whispering, "Soon you die. Soon. Soon!"

Carter knew that the balance had turned against him. He put a final ounce of effort into forcing his knife hand back to its original position, and as it reached that point, as Moultron was for an instant distracted, forced to counter it with an extra effort of his own, Carter let his legs relax, twisted from under him, and rolled off the edge of the bridge.

For a second he dangled over the abyss, and Moultron tried to drop him. It had happened too quickly, and with a swing through space Carter hooked the bridge with his legs and was back again.

He had to grab to pull himself to safety. Moultron, turning, tried to pin him through the chest. Carter rolled. He used his weight and Moultron's weight to carry the machete down. Its blade ended between the slats. He rolled over and their combined weights twisted the handle from Moultron's grasp.

The big man lunged from his knees, trying to get his hands on Carter's throat, and Carter, standing, stunned him with a thrust into the shoulder. Again they struggled.

There was no room for maneuvering. Carter retreated, using his reach, jabbing Moultron with the stiletto as the man came after him.

The knife turned Moultron's body into a bloody

mass. Blood ran across his chest, further soaking what was left of this tattered shirt.

But Moultron would not go down and he would not die. The man was oblivious of everything now, and Carter knew it. He bent, slipped the stiletto into his bush boot, and advanced. When they came together, Carter went to work with his fists.

The change of pace did what the Killmaster wanted. It threw Moultron off his own pace. In a lunging pass Carter managed to tug the briefcase from around the other man's neck and loop an arm through the strap to secure it to his own body.

If anything, it made the man more ferocious. He came on like thunder.

Carter had ceased making any attempt to guard himself. He held a guide rope with his left hand and used it to bring more power into his right. But Moultron kept coming. The bridge's angle steepened. At a point where Carter half turned to gain footing, he lunged.

Carter had anticipated it and planned his response. He fell. He twisted in falling, struck the footway on his back and shoulders, doubled his knees under his chin. It was timed exactly. He let his feet straighten with the suddenness of released springs. He caught Moultron in the belly. He drove him backward.

The big man struck one of the guide ropes with his right shoulder. It turned him halfway around. He screamed and, wild-eyed, made a grab for the footway. He got it and saved himself, and Carter, holding the guide rope behind him with both arms, followed.

He drove the heel and sole of his heavy, water-soaked bush boot into Moultron's face. Moultron still held. Carter braced himself and drove the boot again and again and again until he was blind from exertion and Moultron's face was a shapeless pulp. One could scarcely have told where his nose and eyes and mouth were, but still he held.

Then, suddenly, Carter was being pushed out of the way. Anna bent her middle over the guide rope and held on. Then she went to work with a vengeance on Moultron's fingers.

Carter could only step back and view the macabre sight. As Anna kicked at his fingers she screamed curses at him, and Moultron answered her in kind.

Slowly his fingers lost their grasp on the footway.

Moultron made one more desperate grab. He got hold of the projecting ends of two slats and dug in his fingernails. For a few seconds the strength of his hands held his great weight despite the mist-slick wood, and the thirty- or forty-degree angle at which it dipped.

But the fingers slipped. First a quarter inch at a time, and then more rapidly. His fingertips were torn to shreds. The fingers gave way, and he fell.

Relieved of his weight, the bridge snapped up and swung crazily, almost twisting back on itself. Carter held. His eyes closed, feeling drunk and giddy, he held and held until the movement was an easy rocking.

He opened his eyes. Somehow he still expected Moultron to be there. The bridge was empty. He looked down.

Anna sat, one hand on the rope, the other arm dangling over the side. She was staring down between her knees at the place where Moultron had disappeared into the fog.

Carter got his breath and spoke at last. "Satisfied?"

It was a full minute before her face swiveled up and her cold eyes met his. Her tone was ice when she spoke. "Very."

"Then get on your feet. It ain't over yet. I want to be in Zürich by tomorrow night."

FIFTEEN

Anna was like a zombie through the connecting flights to Zürich and the brief waiting periods in airports making connections. She rarely spoke, and the fierce spark that Carter had seen in her from the first moment he had met her seemed gone.

If she slept at all, Carter didn't see it. She was awake when he slipped off into a catnap, and still awake when he came to again.

At Kloten Airport, they got the VIP treatment through customs even though both of them looked like refugees from a battle zone.

Which, of course, they were.

They were just emerging into the main terminal, when a hand gently but firmly closed on Carter's upper arm.

"Hello, Nick," said a voice softly.

Carter turned quickly and found himself confronted with a pleasant oval face belonging to a man about forty-five years old. The man was wearing a nondescript raincoat and a gray snap-brim hat. From under the hat curled blond, rather frizzy hair into sideburns that were just a trifle long. Crow's feet at the corners of the eyes and lines near the mouth suggested the face was probably most relaxed when it was smiling. It was an agreeable, honest-looking countenance, and it belonged to Amos Mellon, head of AXE station, Zürich.

"Good of you to meet us in person, Amos."

"No problem—you're suddenly a very important person."

"Anna Djumi."

"Miss." Mellon shook Anna's limp hand, did a double take at her vacant stare, and turned back to Carter. "I took a two-bedroom suite for you at the Hotel Zürich. The car is this way."

Mellon got between them and guided them from the terminal. As they emerged from glass doors, a second man, who had apparently been waiting nearby, fell into step behind them.

The car was a nondescript brown sedan. The other man got in front with a driver. Carter, Mellon, and Anna climbed into the back. They had barely settled into the seat when the car lurched from the curb and challenged the Zürich traffic.

They hit Route 4 and the firs and pines of the Zürichberg hills were flying past the windows before Mellon spoke.

"Is that it?" he asked, pointing to the battered briefcase.

"I hope so," Carter replied, passing it over. "I looked through the papers, but I couldn't make sense out of them."

Mellon slid the briefcase between his legs protectively. "There's a team in from Washington. They're standing by. We should know in twenty-four hours if the Poseidon Device is for real."

Carter nodded. "How about the ad?"

"Personals column of both local newspapers and the *Herald Tribune*, just like the lady said. It took a little pressure to get them to run it on such short notice, but we got it done."

"Pletov?"

Mellon's eyes roamed out the window and back.

"They lost him in London, Nick. The guy is like an eel."

"And here, in Zürich?"

"If he got in, he came on skis. We've seen no sign of him. If he's here he's become one of the invisible gnomes."

"Damn," Carter growled, and turned to Anna. "You heard?"

She nodded. "I heard. If the ad ran today, we are to meet him tomorrow afternoon, just the way I told you."

"Is the money ready?" Carter asked Mellon.

"It is," the man replied. "But I don't make any transfers until this is proved genuine." He patted the briefcase. "And Pletov proves he's got a matching set of the plans."

The Zürich is a modern, high-rise hotel on the Limmat River behind the main train station. It has ten lavish penthouse suites. One of these would be their home for the next twenty-four hours.

Mellon passed the briefcase to the man in the front of the sedan, and accompanied them to their rooms.

"We had some clothes and accessories purchased and placed in the closets," he said. "That bedroom is yours."

"Thank you." Without another word, Anna crossed the room, went through the door, and closed it behind her.

Mellon turned to Carter. "Brrrr," he said, mocking a shiver.

"She's been through a lot," Carter said, "but she carried her own weight. I think all the emotion has gone out of her."

Mellon shrugged. "I had ice and your favorite scotch put in your room."

"Thanks. Join me?"

"Thanks, but no, thanks. I've still got your bird, Pletov, to find," he said, and, with a wave, left the suite.

Carter poured himself a healthy shot of scotch, and stripped. After a hot-cold-hot shower, he staggered back to the bedroom and the bottle. A second short drink had the desired effect, and he slipped between the sheets.

It was ten minutes later, maybe more, when he heard the bedroom door open. He opened one eye to see Anna step inside and close it behind her. She was wearing a lacy black nightgown that did wonderful things to what she already had going for her.

Silently, Carter applauded Mellon's taste.

"Are you awake?"

"No," Carter said.

"It's over now."

"No, it isn't," he replied. "Not yet. Not until this time tomorrow."

"Yes." She was by the bed now. "I don't want to sleep alone. Okay?"

"Okay," Carter said, and felt her body join his.

She hadn't taken off the nightgown.

It was just as well. He was asleep before she got completely snuggled against him.

It was a cold, raw day on Lake Zürich. The wind whipped up whitecaps and caused a chop that made the small white lake steamer wallow as it drove its way across the lake.

Carter was glad to stay inside the overheated salon, protected from the chill of the restless gray lake visible through the large viewing window, now almost opaque from the mist and spume.

He and Anna, bundled up in caps, scarves, and heavy coats, were inconspicuous where they sat among the other passengers, loaded with their packages and string bags from a day's shopping in Zürich.

"Where do we go when we land?" Carter asked.

"Up the main street, four blocks to the church, then left. It's a small French restaurant called La Petite Ferme."

Carter chuckled. "Pletov isn't taking any chances."

She merely shrugged.

"What will you do with your money? Where will you go?"

Again she shrugged. "I don't know. I haven't thought beyond . . . Moultron."

She looked away.

The throb of the boat engine lessened. The steamer was heading in toward a dock that lay at the foot of the main street of a small village. The gilt hands of a clock, in the tower of an ivy-covered church in the distance, pointed to noon.

"We're right on time," Carter said, taking her arm. "Let's go."

They descended a broad staircase to the lower deck for disembarking. Side by side they moved into the crowd of departing passengers.

At the bottom of the gangway, they walked the length of the pier and started up the curving incline of the main village street.

"This would be a peaceful place to live," Anna commented, glancing in the shop windows already lighted in the early winter darkness.

"You'd get bored," Carter said.

"Would I?"

"Take my word for it . . . you would."

At the church they turned left into a narrow lane that

ran steeply uphill between Swiss-style half-timbered stucco houses.

La Petite Ferme was quaint and cozy, and reeked of neighborhood charm. Genial laughter and chatty conversation bubbled all around them as they made their way through the small tables to a vacant booth in the rear.

"See him?" Carter murmured.

"No," she replied. "But being the cautious animal that he is, I imagine he is somewhere watching us."

They ordered, more for show than anything else. Carter picked at his food, finally gave up, and just sipped a beer.

Anna did the same, downing two glasses of wine and ordering a third.

At one o'clock Carter got edgy, but tried to be reasonable with his own thoughts and her.

"Was there a contingency? I mean, if he couldn't get to Zürich, was there a fallback, a second time and place to meet?"

Anna shook her head. "No, this is all he told me. This restaurant at noon the day after the ad appeared."

Carter ordered another beer.

At two o'clock he excused himself to go to the men's room. He bypassed the door, heading instead for the rear exit. In the alley he walked a full block around the restaurant.

He spotted nothing, and returned.

Just after three o'clock, he called Amos Mellon.

"He hasn't shown up."

"I told you. If he was in Zürich, I think we would have known about it."

Carter had an idea. "Have you got any way of checking the account, his account? I'd like to know how much of our money is left in it."

"I'll try," Mellon replied, "but you know Swiss bankers."

Carter hung up and returned to the table. Anna was staring off into nothing, into midair, with a crazy, lop-sided grin on her face.

"What's with you?"

"We've been taken."

"What?"

She laughed out loud. "As you Americans so color-fully put it, we've been suckered. He isn't showing up. He was lying all the time."

"What makes you so sure?"

"I'm not, not really. But I have a feeling. He's just not coming, that's all."

By five o'clock Carter agreed with her. He picked up the check and put on his coat.

A jovial, fat little woman sat on a high stool behind a cash register by the door. Behind her were little cubby-holes in a large cabinet. Each slot had a letter of the alphabet just below it.

Carter knew what it was. Every small village in Europe has a café or restaurant where its regular pa-trons could leave messages for each other.

It would be like Pletov, Carter thought.

"Excuse me, madame . . ."

"Oui?"

"I am an American. My name is Carter, Nick Carter. We were supposed to meet a friend here this afternoon. He didn't arrive. I wonder if there was any message?"

The woman swiveled on her stool. Her hand darted into the cubbyhole marked "C" and came out with a small package.

"Oui. Carter, Nick Carter. Here you are."

"Merci, madame."

He left his change on the counter and they hit the

street. In less than half a block he had unwrapped the package. Inside was a cassette tape.

"Pletov?"

"You know it," Carter growled. "Let's find a store that sells tape recorders."

They found one at the foot of the street.

The clerk thought Carter was slightly daft. "But, mein Herr, for another fifty francs you can buy."

"I don't want to buy it, I only want to use it for five minutes . . . in your office."

The clerk shrugged and guided them into a tiny office. He set the portable recorder/player on a desk and left.

Carter pushed in the tape and hit the "play" button.

In seconds they heard Pletov's voice.

"Well, Carter, if you are listening to this, you're still alive. Congratulations. Also, because of your expertise in these matters, I am guessing that Anna Djumi has also survived the ordeal unscathed.

"Now to business.

"I am afraid, Carter, that I have lied. I do not have a second set of plans for the device. I am afraid I have never had them. The reason for my little deception, I should think, is obvious. I, like Anna, wanted revenge. I also wanted a decent amount of money for my labors.

"You have provided that, and I thank you.

"Since I do not have the plans, I cannot expect you to pay the second half of the agreed-upon sum. I, however, am satisfied with the amount I do have.

"You, I should think, will also be satisfied, since I assume Moultron is dead and you have the only set of written plans.

"I consider the amount of money you have already given me, earned. After all, through Anna, I did lead you to Moultron.

"Now for you, dear Anna.

"Since you have gotten the revenge you so desired, I am sure you will be amenable to a lesser amount of cash than was our original agreement. On that basis I have transferred one hundred thousand dollars into your account at Suisse Crédit Nationale. With your meager needs I am sure you will find that satisfactory.

"Now, to the both of you, I bid *adieu* forever, and I do hope that this will close the book on our business."

The tape went silent. Carter stared at it silently while, beside him, Anna laughed, low in her throat and slightly hysterical.

"You think being shorted nine hundred grand is funny?"

She shrugged and managed to control her laughter. "I never trusted Pletov from the beginning, so I really haven't lost."

"Then the money doesn't mean anything?"

The smile disappeared and the face went hard. The eyes again flashed with the same fire he had seen when she had talked of Moultron.

"Of course the money means something. It means everything, an escape from the kind of life I have had to lead. It means I could go anywhere and do anything I wanted. Of course it means something, but I am not a person who cries over what is past. I have been outsmarted by Pletov." Here she shrugged again. "I'll accept my winnings, or losses, and play at another table."

Carter studied her for a moment. "Do you really have an account at Suisse Crédit Nationale?"

She nodded. "Pletov set it up for me right after he found me. It's only a few thousand. He said it was for expenses until it came time to go after Moultron."

Carter pushed the telephone toward her. "Check the amount on deposit."

Anna got the number and called. After a short wait she was put through to an officer. She gave the proper code name for the account and the number. Seconds later she had the figure and hung up.

"One hundred and twelve thousand," she said. "At least he did that much." Then it dawned on her. "What did you think, that I knew about this all the time? Did you think I was going to play it out with you, and then slink off to meet him?"

"The thought had entered my mind," Carter said, "if there had been no deposit."

"Me? That boor's mistress?" she flared. "I would think you knew me better than that by now!"

"And you should know by now that I don't trust anyone. C'mon, let's get back to the hotel."

They shunned the ferry and took a cab around the lake. Forty-five minutes later they entered the suite.

Amos Mellon was waiting for them. Carter told him the basics of the tape and handed it over.

The other man didn't seem too perturbed. "No matter. We've got what we wanted."

Carter sighed with relief. "You mean the stuff is good?"

Melon nodded. "According to the experts, it's as good as gold, and worth more. Evidently, Moultron hit on a combination of magnetic and laser sensors to form a new theory of SAR—synthetic aperture radar. All his notes and equations on the test results point to a sure thing. Believe me, Nick, they were elated."

Carter flopped in a chair and accepted the drink Mellon had made. Anna stood to the side, uninterested.

"There can be no reversals, no doubts?"

"None," Mellon replied, "according to the team who did the evaluation. They're already on their way back to Washington, as happy as kids on Christmas morning."

Carter sipped his drink and glanced at Anna. She met his stare but said nothing with her eyes.

"Amos?"

"Yeah?"

"You haven't released the rest of the money yet, have you?"

"No, why?"

Carter pushed a blank pad and a pen across the table to Anna. "Write down your account number."

She did, without emotion, and Carter handed it to Mellon. "I don't think the agency would disagree that it's still a cheap investment."

Mellon studied them both, and made a decision. "How much?"

"Nine very big ones."

Mellon closed his briefcase and pocketed the slip of paper. "I think it can be arranged."

"It's the Suisse Crédit Nationale."

"I'll take care of it right away."

Anna stepped forward and gently placed her hand on Carter's shoulder. "You would do that for me?"

"You earned it."

He actually saw tears in her eyes, and it amazed him. He didn't think she was capable.

"Thank you," she said in a husky voice, and turned. She walked directly into her bedroom and closed the door behind her.

There were a few seconds of awkward silence between the two men, and then Mellon headed for the door.

"I'll check you in with Washington. Try to get your report in within the next twenty-four hours."

"Will do," Carter replied.

The door closed behind Mellon, and Carter could hear the shower running in Anna's room. He cracked the door an inch and peered through. There was a bag, already packed, on the bed, and clothes ready for travel laid out neatly beside it.

Sipping his drink, he moved into the bathroom. She was just stepping from the shower.

"Where will you go?"

"I don't know. Somewhere I've never been before, where no one knows me and I know no one. Somewhere I can forget all this."

"I usually have a few weeks between assignments. Want some company?"

Now she stared frankly at him, assessing his words. Carter could sense the emotion in her eyes and the thoughts charging through her beautiful head.

"A few weeks?" she said at last.

"Yeah."

"And then off again, somewhere else in the world to do the same thing all over again?"

Carter dropped his eyes from hers and studied the melting ice in his glass. "There always seems to be another Moultron."

"Not for me," Anna said, lightly brushing her lips across his check and moving past him into the bedroom.

She stood with her back to him, dressing. It was in the set of her spine, in the way her hands moved, and in the quick tosses of her hair as her head moved.

As far as Anna was concerned, for her the wars were over.

Carter headed for the door. He was nearly there when the phone rang. He headed on into the living room of the suite and answered it there.

"Yeah, Carter here."

"Nick, Amos . . . news."

"Good or bad?" Carter asked, draining his glass.

"Very bad, I'm afraid. It seems our bird, Pletov, is lying all around."

Carter froze. "How so?"

"Euro-intercept picked up some high-level traffic early this morning out of the Russian embassy in Paris to Madrid. One piece was red-flagged and rushed to Hawk in Washington. It—and his comments—were waiting on my desk when I got in."

"Pletov?"

"You guessed it. He's making a deal with his old buddies. It seems he's agreed to a Kremlin offer for some goods he's peddling."

A chill went up Carter's spine and his knuckles went white around the empty glass. "The Poseidon plans."

"The message didn't state that specifically, but it would stand to reason. It looks like your boy is going for the whole nine yards after all, and probably lifetime immunity from the KGB."

"Is that it?"

"Not quite. Maybe one lead. The meet for the exchange is going down about this time Thursday."

"Forty-eight hours," Carter hissed.

"Give or take. The big man wants you to try and find him or head him off at the meet. We'll have a tail on every Red operative in Madrid to give you a hand, if it comes to that."

"Get me on a flight."

"I've already done it. You leave at seven-forty tonight for Madrid."

The line went dead and Carter slammed the phone back to the cradle. "Shit."

"What is it?"

He turned. She was in the doorway, dressed now in a white suit with a soft blue scarf at her throat.

"Pletov," he growled, and told her the rest in short, terse sentences as he headed for his own room. "I'm heading for Madrid."

It took him fifteen minutes to change and pack. When he finished, he carried his bag into the sitting room.

Anna was there, sitting on the arm of a chair smoking a cigarette. Her own packed bag was on the floor by the chair.

"I thought you'd be gone by now," he said tightly, with more anger than he really felt.

"Touchy, aren't we?"

"Sorry." He moved around the room, making sure he had everything.

"Spain, huh?"

"Yeah, somewhere in Spain, but it's a damn big country."

"Maybe I can help."

He stopped. "I'm in the water with no life preserver."

"There is a woman. I think she used to be a singer. She is married to a blind man, a piano player. I also think that a long time ago, in Lisbon, she worked for Pletov. Maybe she was his woman."

"What about her?"

"It was this woman who found me for Pletov. It was she who met with me several times. I suppose she was, what you call, feeling me out for Pletov. When she was satisfied that I could go through with everything, it was she who gave me Pletov's initial instructions."

Carter mulled this over. "If she was that close to Pletov once, she still could be."

"Perhaps."

"If he's in hiding and wants to stay there, he'll need a runner, someone to do his contacting for him."

Carter was thinking aloud, ironing out this new wrinkle. Anna realized it and just shrugged or nodded at his musings without commenting herself.

"Do you have a name?" he asked at last.

"Not for her, but I recognized her husband. Years ago, he gained some fame as a composer. I've seen his picture on sheet music. Pedro Silvera."

Carter dived for the phone. In seconds he had Amos Mellon back on the line. He gave the AXE agent Silvera's name and requested every piece of information the Spanish could supply. Particularly, he wanted current whereabouts.

He was about to hang up, when Anna grasped his arm.

"Have Mr. Mellon get another seat on that flight."

"You're sure?"

"I am sure. I want to see this all the way through . . . now."

Carter relayed the request to Mellon and replaced the phone.

"When you met with this couple . . ."

"Yes?"

"Did you give them any hint at any time that you knew who they were?"

"No. Pletov had given the woman explicit instructions to keep her identity a secret."

"All the more reason," Carter said, "that he probably planned to use her again down the road."

The phone rang again. It was Amos Mellon.

"They just intercepted again, Nick, out of Paris to Madrid. The deal is on."

"We're on our way."

SIXTEEN

The information they needed was waiting for them in Madrid.

Pedro Silvera had been ardently anti-Franco and was a member of the Spanish Communist party, as was his wife, Risa. Years before, they had both immigrated to Portugal to escape arrest by the Franco regime.

While there was no connection with Pletov established on file, there were convincing coincidences. The Silveras were in Lisbon about the same time as Pletov when the Russian was attached to the Russian embassy in Lisbon.

It was just after the Silveras moved back to Spain from Portugal that Pletov defected. His defection was through Spain, and it was arranged by an unknown Spanish woman who played liaison.

It all fit. Now all they had to do was find Pedro and Risa Silvera. The only address the Spanish authorities had was a post office box in Cartagena, on the Costa Blanca. This had been obtained through Rivera's music publisher, who still sent the composer small royalty checks.

The fastest way was a commuter flight from Madrid to Valencia. They stayed the night there, and the following morning hired a car and driver to take them down the coast to Cartagena.

The man drove like a person possessed, with one hand

on the wheel and the other on the horn button. When he wasn't screaming abuse at other drivers or meandering tourists, he hummed flamenco through his nose.

Conversation or contact was impossible with the constant lurch of the vehicle as the driver avoided potholes. They separated to sit silently in the corners of the rear seat, hanging desperately to the arm slings. They drove through barren plains, pine forests dark against the brilliant sunshine, red tilled earth, and ancient olive trees.

Speed was never slackened, even when they roared through dusty seaside villages with a few patched boats pulled up on the beach.

It was nearly noon when they reached Cartagena. Carter had booked a room from Valencia. The driver knew it. He roared through the greater part of the city and back out the southern side. Suddenly the car lurched to the left. They climbed a driveway for fifty yards, and came to an abrupt stop in front of an immense stone building.

The driver swiveled in his seat, taking off his dark glasses and smiling brilliantly. "Hotel La Mancha," he said. "Good time, eh?"

"And in one piece," Anna murmured, sighing with relief.

Carter paid him, adding a liberal tip, and a young boy took their bags.

The hotel graced a sheer cliff running straight up from the sea. Rough stone, doors of carved wood studded with brass, with the grounds a large olive grove.

In the room, Carter rechecked with Washington, Amos Mellon, and their Madrid contact.

Nothing new.

"What now?" Anna asked.

"The bars," Carter replied. "In Spain, everyone drinks, eats, and socializes. The Riveras sound like a bit of an odd couple. Someone will know them."

"We just ask?" she said with surprise.

"Not exactly. We go in separately. Your Spanish is adequate and you look less threatening than I do, so you do the inquiring. You're a musician and writer. You're putting together a book on little-known Spanish popular composers."

Her face screwed up. "You think that will work?"

"It's as good as anything else. Let's go."

They started at the southern end of the beach and worked their way north, choosing only the bars that advertised some kind of live music in the evenings.

Anna played her part well, amassing names of local musicians and jotting them in a notebook as if they were gold. By midafternoon they were bloated with wine and food and they had no results.

Carter was about to give up for the siesta hour, when they hit a place called La Estrella. There was nothing different about it—dark, even with the glare of the mid-afternoon sun outside, a few fishermen and a tourist or two for customers, a tired bartender, and a ferret-faced artist with a cigarette pasted between his lips in one corner near the door. The artist pitched Anna when she entered, and Carter close behind. When they both declined, he relit his cigarette and went back to the comic book he had been reading.

They had established a routine, Carter to the bar and a beer, Anna to a table and a glass of wine.

It didn't take long. Anna did her routine with the waitress, pushed a little when the woman didn't seem to have answers, and gave up.

After a couple of sips of the wine she looked at Carter and shook her head. He nodded.

She dropped a bill on the bar and headed for the door. Carter prepared to do the same, when Anna suddenly stopped near the artist. When she spoke, it was loud enough for Carter to hear.

"Are all these for sale?"

"*Si, señorita*. All oil originals, and for sale. Which one you like? I make you good price."

Anna began going through the canvases. Carter took his beer and edged down the bar until he could see as well as hear. He watched her thumb through seascapes, landscapes, and portraits until she finally chose one.

When she did, she held it up so Carter could see. It was a portrait of a hawk-faced man with a graying beard and a high forehead. He wore dark glasses and was seated at a piano with a cloud of smoke swirling around his head.

"This intrigues me," Anna said.

"Ah, the señnorita has very fine taste. This is nice painting. Only three thousands pesetas."

"I think I'll take it. Uh, where was it painted?"

"Here, señorita, in Cartagena."

"Yes, but where?"

The little artist seemed perplexed. He took the painting from her hands and held it close to his face, staring at it for a long time through squinted eyes.

Carter could tell from the frown of concentration on his face that, if remembering the place where he had painted the picture meant making the sale, he was bound and determined that he would remember.

Anna stood at his shoulder riffling bills and prodding him. Finally he turned in glee toward her, a wide smile on his face.

"Ah, I remember . . . La Canción del Mar!"

"You're sure?"

"I am sure, señorita. Positive!"

Anna bought the painting and left with it under her arm. Carter waited a few minutes and followed.

"Luck?"

"A lot of luck," she replied. "It's Pedro Silvera."

"Let's find La Canción del Mar!"

The Song of the Sea was right on the beach. It was a run-down kind of place that few tourists would ever risk going into, even in daylight. The floor was filthy, and there was a stage for local talent at the end of the long room.

The place wasn't crowded. A couple of drunks at the bar were arguing over a lottery ticket. Except for them, Anna and Carter had the place to themselves.

This time they came in and sat at the bar together.

The barman was fat and had a scar to one side of his face that puckered like a dimple when he smiled.

Carter ordered wine, and when it came, turned the painting around so the barman could see it. He went into the spiel Ann had already been using about writing a book.

The barman looked bored, until Carter produced a roll of bills and began peeling them his way. When the Killmaster reached a stack to the barman's liking, he spoke.

"The painting is of Pedro Silvera. One in a while he will come in very late at night, always very drunk, and he will play sad Portuguese fado there, at the piano."

"Is Silvera still here, in Cartagena?" Carter asked.

"*Sí,* I believe he is," the man replied, eyeing the wad in Carter's hand.

A few more bills passed over the bar.

Slowly and explicitly, the barman gave them directions to the house of Pedro Silvera.

They followed the paving stones of a ramp to steps that led down to the beach. The house was a small stucco building at the bottom of the steps, backed up to a stand of rushes.

As they reached the door, Carter mopped the back of his neck with a limp handkerchief. Inside they heard the tinkling of a piano. Anna knocked.

"Who is there?" a hoarse voice called from inside.

Anna explained that she was a writer, that she had a photographer with her, and that they would like to interview Pedro Silvera.

"The door is open."

They entered. Silvera, his hair completely gray now, sat at a piano. Near to his right hand was a half-full bottle of red wine.

One glance told them both that Pedro Silvera was very drunk.

"This interview . . . you will pay?"

Anna glanced at Carter, who nodded. "If the story is complete, I think we could pay, yes," she said.

"Then ask your questions."

Anna was good. She went halfway around the moon before she came to the point.

"And your wife, Risa—I would also like to interview her."

Silvera's lips curled into a snarl. "My wife is a whore. She has always been a whore!"

"Then, Señor Silvera, you and your wife are no longer together?"

"Now and then," he shrugged. "Right now she is with one of her lovers. I don't know when she will be back."

Anna did her best to get more out of him, but at every mention of his wife, Silvera would go into a tantrum.

Finally he demanded money before he would say more. Carter gave the man several bills, and explained that he would like to take some photographs, of the house and Silvera.

The man shrugged and drank. Anna asked more inane questions while Carter prowled.

It took him nearly a half hour to find anything, but when he did he was pretty sure it was the jackpot. Underneath old clothes in a chest was a stack of brochures for villas and farmhouses for sale. Each of them was listed through the Cordez Agency in Cartagena.

Two of the sheets looked more thumbed-over than the others, and had circles penciled around the pictures.

Carter took them all and returned to Anna and Silvera.

Another ten minutes and Anna had it skillfully wrapped up. Outside, Carter hustled her back to the main street.

"You found something?"

"Yeah. You're going to pay a visit to the Cordez Agency."

According to the address on the brochure, it was on the other side of town. They cabbed it.

"Play it very cool, like a customer. I'll meet you in that bar on the corner."

"What are you going to do?"

"Arrange transportation."

About three blocks away he found a row of stores. Carter bought a cheap pair of field glasses, mechanic's overalls, a helmet, and a pair of goggles. He also got directions to the nearest motorcycle shop.

It was another four blocks away.

He went in. A dozen battered scooters were parked in a wooden rack. Flat in the oily dirt, a man was tinkering with the rear end of an ancient Citroën. Hearing Carter enter, he rolled over, propping himself with the mallet in his hand.

"Buenos tardes, señor. What can I do for you?"

Carter explained what he wanted. The Spaniard clambered to his feet, wiping grease from his face with a greasy rag.

"All are superb machines!" He waved a hand at the rack. "Some are still better than others. For how long, señor?"

"Three weeks."

"Three weeks!" The garage proprietor tried to hide his pleasure. He lifted a scooter from the rack, bouncing it on its wheels, flicking the rusting chrome. "Here is a magnificent *moto.* For three weeks, I am willing to make a concession. Six thousand pesetas." He dabbed his nose, using the rag as a screen from behind which he watched Carter's reaction. *"Por Dios!"* he said suddenly. "And I make you a gift of the gasoline!"

Carter tried the controls. The price the man asked for the scooter's hire was high. But the brakes worked and the tiny motor buzzed like an angry hornet. He gave the man six one-thousand-peseta bills.

"And the señor's address?" The man was at his desk. Head at an angle, he wrote in flowery style on an invoice.

"Barron," said Carter, giving the man the name on the ID he was currently using. "Care of the British consulate, Valencia."

"You have papers, señor? Some means of identification?"

"With me, no," Carter said pleasantly. "If you insist, I will fetch them."

"You are staying in Cartagena?"

"Yes, at the Hotel La Mancha."

The man picked up the telephone. Two minutes later

he was satisfied. "It will not be necessary, señor. Please sign here."

Carter scrawled a signature on the paper, and rode the scooter back to the bar

Anna was waiting.

"Well?"

She placed one of the dog-eared brochures in front of him. "I wanted to look at this one very badly. It was purchased six weeks ago with a down payment from a Swiss bank. Three days ago, the remainder was paid for in cash, also from a Swiss bank."

Carter picked up the brochure. "Cabo de Palos."

"It's a point about fifteen miles north of here."

"I can find it," he said, folding the paper and putting it in his jacket. "You go back to the hotel and check out."

"And then?"

"Dump my bag anywhere. I won't be needing it."

Anna paused before she spoke. "You're sure you don't want me along?"

"Very sure. You've done enough."

She shrugged and started toward the door. Suddenly she paused and turned. "Nick . . ."

"Yeah?"

"Those weeks you mentioned . . ."

"Yeah?"

"I'll be at the Mamounia in Marrakesh."

Carter smiled. "It's a date."

SEVENTEEN

Carter located the drive from the road down to the renovated farmhouse. He rode past it a mile, hid the scooter, and made his way back along the beach. When he was within a few hundred yards, he moved off the beach into a stand of trees. There he moved forward again until he hit a clearing on high ground that looked right down over his objective.

He put the glasses on it, cupping his hands over the lens to avoid telltale reflection. The cheap binoculars were not powerful enough to bring detail into sharp focus. But he could see a long white house with a red tile roof and a truck parked in front of it. Behind the truck was a newish Mercedes sedan. Between the truck and the sedan, two men moved, loading empty crates.

Carter moved twenty feet deeper into the trees. Finding a spot, he propped himself against a tree, watching and waiting. About ten minutes later, the men finished their work, and he could hear the sound of the engine. He dropped to his stomach again, elbows square on the ground, training the glasses on the clearing.

The truck turned, then roared up the lane toward him. He lay where he was, still, as it passed.

It was then that he noticed the name on the truck's door, of a local furniture store, and smiled to himself.

184

Comrade Pletov had moved in.

Carter started to work his way through the trees, keeping the setting sun behind him. There were no birds to raise a squawk in sudden alarm. Indeed, he saw nothing that lived but the tree spiders. They were all around him, and after a while he tired of brushing their sticky webs from his face. For twenty minutes he moved like that, every sense alert, straining himself for the unexpected. The only sound was the faint crunch his own body made as he moved.

Near at hand, he heard women's voices. He stopped, then moved on again, cautiously, checking every few yards. When he neared the house, he went down flat, wriggling like a snake.

The trees were thinner now. The sun shone through the boughs, patterning the ground around him with shadow.

The clearing with its main house and outbuildings was thirty yards away. He crawled nearer, wiping the sweat from his eyes. His back and legs itched in a hundred places. But he kept his even breathing shallow in the attempt to remain hidden.

The walls of the house were white and thick, broken with deep shadow where open shutters swung a little. Fifty yards away was a cement block building with a flat roof where washing hung on a taut line. There was a ladder against the smaller house. A young woman stood on it, slapping whitewash on the wall. A second woman held the ladder. Their voices were shrill and clear in the still air.

When Carter was sure that they couldn't spot him, he got to his feet and moved around to the front of the house.

A great pepper tree stood before the front door. There was a patch of grass, green under a hose. Flower beds in front of the windows blazed yellow and crimson. Beyond them, in the full glare of the fierce sun, Pletov lay on a rubber mattress. He was stripped to shorts, his face turned upward, both arms outstretched in the position of a man crucified.

Instinctively, Carter's fingers found the butt of the Luger. He tensed—as if sure the other must smell his presence. Pletov's eyes stayed shut. With infinite care, Carter started to haul his weight up the bole of a tree. Fifteen feet above, a thick branch pointed at the house, like an outstretched finger. He straddled it, his back against the trunk of the tree. He was thirty yards away from the still figure.

As he watched, a woman came from the house. She was beautiful, neither young nor old, with a dark, chiseled face. She wore tight-fitting slacks, and her full, high breasts were prominent in a peasant blouse.

She stopped a few paces from Pletov. "I am ready to go."

Pletov opened his eyes and rolled his head toward her. "Good. They will come to your suite at the hotel. When they produce proof of the deposit, call me at the Almeria number. I will give them what they want there."

"I don't like it."

"Risa, Risa . . ."

She ran to him, her face sullen, her mouth petulant. "Why should I have to face them in person? What if they keep me to get to you?"

"They won't."

"How do you know they won't?" she cried, her eyes

flashing. "It is always you who are safe . . . in the background. I've run all over the world for you, and now you tell me that I must still live like this!" Her hand went in an arc toward the house.

"Do as you are told, Risa."

"I won't! With all the money you are getting, why can't we live somewhere civilized? Why can't we—"

Pletov's left hand grabbed her ankle. He pulled her to the ground beside him. Then he slashed at her cheeks with the palm of his hand. Twice he jolted her head, first to the left and then the right.

"Shut up!" he snarled. "We will stay in this place because it is safe, for as long as it takes. When it is safe, you can leave your sot of a husband for good and we will go to where we can spend the money. But for now we will do it my way!"

She crouched where she had fallen, holding her cheeks. She looked bewildered. Tears came and she hid her face in her arms.

"They will never let you live, the Americans or the Russians," she sobbed.

"When they realize that they have a stalemate, they will forget about me and the embarrassment that I have caused them. Now go, and take those two chattering women with you. Leave them off in Cartagena."

He pulled her to her feet and pushed her toward the house.

As they disappeared, Carter dug his nails into the rough bark of the tree and waited.

There was no sound from inside for a quarter hour. Then the woman came to the doorway carrying a small bag.

Pletov appeared. He had put on a garish yellow shirt

and white trousers. A white scarf was around his neck.

He escorted Risa Silvera to the car. The two servant women got in the back.

"Call me the moment you are checked into the Chamartin."

The woman said something Carter couldn't hear, and the engine roared to life.

The car wheeled and accelerated up the drive between the trees. Pebbles scattered and dust hung in the air. When it settled, Pletov walked toward the low, cement block building and went inside.

The house stood empty, the dark open door an invitation. Carter dropped to the ground, careless now about noise. Once he was in the house, he would be able to see the other building from one of the back windows. He ran through the trees and out to the clearing. In the shade of the pepper tree, he stopped. The weathered door was wide, revealing walls two feet thick. He could see a tiled floor, littered with excelsior. The load the truck had brought had been left in the hall. Chests with iron handles. A refrigerator. Carved headboards for beds. Beyond the litter of furniture, a wide staircase was dark against the white walls.

He counted the windows. There were eight above and eight below. Bent iron made graceful grilles in front of each. At night, the heavy door would be shut, the giant key turned, the bolts rammed home. Whatever Pletov had to protect would be as safe as if in a bank.

He crossed the green and moved through the open door. At the far end of the hall, sun shone through an open window. There were flies buzzing in the shaft of light, and a clock ticked in a room to his left.

He was in a large kitchen with a tiled floor. The walls

were bright with copper pans and the side door was open.

Suddenly he heard the roar of an engine, and from behind the outbuilding came a Jaguar. Pletov was driving. He halted in the center of the clearing, got out, and headed for the house.

Carter moved into the great room. As he did, he ejected the clip from the Luger and thumbed out all the shells. Then he shoved it back home, leaving only the one shell still in the chamber.

He moved into the darkness of a corner just as Pletov entered, his hands in his pockets, whistling.

"Just keep them right there," Carter hissed.

Pletov stopped. A ripple of tenseness went up his spine, and then he turned slowly.

"You do amaze me, Carter. How?"

"It doesn't make any difference. You know why I'm here."

"I haven't the foggiest, I assure you."

The thin smile stayed on Pletov's face as he raised his chin slightly.

"The plans, Pletov. You should have been satisfied with what you had . . . went through with the deal."

"I told you on the tape . . ."

Carter's finger tightened on the trigger. He stepped back and fired, aiming over the other man's shoulder. Glass splintered and acrid smoke trickled from the barrel of the gun. Carter raised it a second time.

"I'm a good shot, Pletov. Next one goes into your right kneecap."

Pletov moved for the first time, loosening the scarf at his neck. He wrinkled his nose against the cordite fumes, coughing slightly.

"Why do you think I lied on the tape?"

Carter told him. It was like the air coming out of a balloon.

"As usual, my fellow countrymen can be trusted to foul up even the smallest detail. Intercepts . . . by God."

"Give me the plans, Pletov."

"And get myself killed? Surely you jest! Mind if I have a drink?"

"Go ahead." Pletov moved to a sideboard and Carter moved in behind him.

"I suppose you were lurking outside and heard Risa and myself?"

"That's right."

Pletov sighed. "If I do, can we revert to our former deal?"

"No," Carter growled. "Too late for that now." He placed the muzzle of the Luger against the back of Pletov's head. "My guess is that the plans are here, Pletov, somewhere in the house. You've got five seconds to tell me. You don't tell me, I shoot you anyway, and burn the damn thing down around your corpse."

The man was fast, even faster than Carter would have given him credit for being.

He came up and under Carter's arm with one elbow, and smashed the Killmaster's forearm with his other hand.

The Luger clattered to the floor.

Carter made a halfhearted grab for it, but Pletov was, of course, faster.

"Now, damn you, we'll see who is going to die!"

Carter was on his knees, rubbing his left forearm. "Silly, isn't it?"

"What is?"

"What we're doing. I was going to kill you for a few

scraps of paper. Now you're going to kill me for a few rubles.''

Pletov's grin was more like a leer. "A great many rubles, Carter, converted soon into Swiss francs.''

Carter matched the man's grin and slowly got to his feet. "Then this wasn't a wild-goose chase. You do have a second set of plans for the device.''

"Right there.''

Carter followed his outstretched left arm. A slide projector was set up on a small table. Beside it were two boxes of slides.

"By this time tomorrow night, I will have handed those boxes over to a man in Almeria, and my Swiss accounts will be groaning from the weight of all the money they will be holding.''

Carter quit rubbing his arm and started for Pletov.

Shock was all over the man's face. "Stop! Do you want to die so soon, you fool?''

Carter kept coming.

Pletov fired. When the hammer fell on an empty chamber, he fired again, and again.

Carter saw the rage in his face turn to terror just before his fist smashed into Pletov's nose.

Blood spurted, and a howl of pain erupted from Pletov's throat. He slashed out with the Luger, trying to hit Carter's head.

But the Killmaster wasn't there. He was behind Pletov. When the man realized it and turned, Carter chopped the Luger from his grasp and hit him twice in the gut. As he doubled over, Carter's knee came up into his face.

He went down and rolled.

"A deal is a deal, Pletov. You should have stuck with the one I gave you.''

Pletov came up with a chair. He swung it at Carter's side and missed. Carter stepped in and finished him, knocking him cold.

He took a few minutes to get his breath, and then dragged the unconscious body into one of the bedrooms. Carefully, he bound and gagged Pletov. When he was positive the man could not get himself free, he returned to the great room and found the telephone.

AXE Madrid answered on the first ring.

"The meeting is at the Chamartin Hotel, Madrid. The contact there is a woman named Risa Silvera. You can start putting the word out that Pletov is in a farmhouse called Casa Peru in Cabo de Palos, Spain. I'm sure they'll love to hear his side of it."

He hung up and gathered the two boxes of slides.

Ten minutes later he was on the scooter headed back to Cartegena.

By morning, the slides would be on their way to Washington and Carter would be on his way to Marrakesh.

He didn't want to think what the KGB boys would do to Pletov when they broke into the farmhouse and found him.

Or maybe he did want to think of it.

As he rode along, Carter started whistling.

DON'T MISS THE NEXT NEW
NICK CARTER SPY THRILLER

THE ANDROPOV FILE

It was nearly a mile further to the logging camp road. Carter hit it full tilt, and charged up it under an umbrella of tall, leafless trees. One hundred, two hundred, three hundred yards of narrow, winding road . . . and nothing.

"Come on, come on!" he hissed. "Where the hell . . ."

And then they burst into a huge clearing and Carter began snapping the lights off and on.

Except for a couple of big logging trucks and a bulldozer, the place looked abandoned and ghostly. There were several buildings leaning as if they would wobble and fall over in the next big storm.

In less than two minutes Carter had crisscrossed and spun the car around the clearing several times, making a mess of his own tracks.

Then he spun the car around and backed it under a wooden overhead. He killed the lights and engine, and jumped out. Nina was right behind him, calling to her brother.

"Up here!"

They looked. He was half in, half out of a second-story window, a handgun glinting at the end of both arms.

"We're blown!" Carter shouted. "Get down here!"

Lithely, Kadinskov dropped to the ground and ran to join them. "What is it?"

"They had Nina fingered, probably trailed us all the way from Milan. Chances are their job was to take you out if their agent on the train missed."

"How many?"

"Three, on motorcycles. Nina, you drive. Joseph, in the passenger seat."

"What are you going to do?" Nina asked, her brother already climbing into the car.

"Lead them away from the road."

"No, Nick, you've got to come with us!" she cried.

He ignored her. "You've got papers to get you to Italy. You know where to pick up new papers there. I'll buy you time here."

Suddenly she was against him, her lips pressed to his. "Thank you, Nick."

He practically shoved her into the driver's seat.

"Don't start the engine until you hear the first shot. When you do, go like hell, hit the road, and don't look back. Joseph, take good care of her."

"I will. And . . . thank you."

Carter turned and ran down the lane as fast as his legs would carry him, unholstering Wilhelmina.

A hundred yards short of the road he heard the engines. At fifty he heard them cut off, and hit the trees. Ten yards in, he stopped and dropped into a crouch.

It could have been an hour. Actually, it was about two minutes.

The snow was about a foot deep with a hard crust on top. It was impossible for them to be quiet. They were easy to spot by sound. One man was leading point, near the lane, on Carter's side. The other two were about twenty yards behind him, one on each side of the road.

Carter narrowed his eyes, straining them in the darkness.

And then he saw him, his helmet discarded, coming upright, the muzzle of his machine pistol moving from side to side.

Carter was on one knee, motionless, the Luger straight out from his shoulder in both hands.

He waited until the man was less than ten yards from him, and fired twice.

All three machine pistols barked at the same time, one in the air as the dying man fell, and the other two in Carter's direction.

But he was already flat on the ground, his eyes darting around a rotten log.

They were moving as they fired, trying to outflank him.

Then the firing stopped and all of them, hunter and hunted alike, heard the car roaring down the lane.

The two men reacted fast. One of them fired short bursts in Carter's direction to hold him down while the other sprinted back toward the road to head off the car.

Carter could not see either one of them, nor could he hear them now over the chaos. He did hear the car hit high gear and then hurtle around the last bend and straighten out for its run to the road.

Both men forgot about Carter now and tried to find the range on the car.

Then Nina showed her guts. She turned on the headlights. They illuminated one of the men dead center in the road. He was just bringing up his machine pistol when Carter emptied the rest of Wilhelmina's clip into him.

Five seconds later Nina hit him, sending his lifeless body into the trees. The car went on, veered into the road, rocked dangerously, and was gone.

Across the lane, Carter could hear the last man running for the road himself. The Killmaster guessed he was heading for the place where they had hidden the motorcycles.

Jamming a fresh clip into the butt of the Luger, Carter darted through the trees, pretty sure that the third man had figured out the whole scam.

When he heard the man kick the machine to life, he broke from the trees and ran full out. He was certain his prey would be intent on the car now, and could care less about who the shooter in the trees had been or where he was.

The Killmaster hit the end of the lane just as the bike roared out of the trees to his left. He got off two shots, both wild, and dived out of the way.

A stump just below the surface of the snow hit the barrel of the Luger, knocking it from his grasp. He rolled to the side just as the bike swung around and came for him.

It was Duval, and the machine pistol was slung over his shoulder. At that point, Duval wasn't interested in Carter. He wanted the occupants of the car that was long gone down the road.

Carter got to his feet just as the machine got to him. He treated the handlebars as if they were the horns of a charging bull and went right over the top of them, managing to get his arms around Duval's head and his shoulder in the man's face.

And that's the way they sailed, crazily, down the road, before the front wheel hit a slick spot and the bike went over.

Carter went to the side, sliding into the snow on his chest. Duval managed to get his leg from beneath the skidding machine and roll free. He was just unslinging the machine pistol when Carter hit him at the knees in a flying block. With a howl of pain, Duval went down and the gun went sliding across the road to disappear in a snowbank.

They were both up and at each other at once. Carter sidestepped, but Duval countered, getting his arms around the Killmaster's middle.

The intent was obvious. If he could get his hands high enough and keep his body low, he could snap Carter's spine like a twig.

Around and around they danced, suddenly tripping over the still-running motorcycle lying in the middle of the road on its side. Carter managed to keep his balance as the other man rolled free. On the way down, Carter brought his knee up into Duval's face.

It didn't put him out, but it made him good and fuzzy.

They were on opposite sides of the purring motorcycle. Carter was on his knees, waiting. When Duval started coming for him again, Carter reached out and locked his fingers behind the other man's neck. Then he pulled down, jamming Duval's face into the red-hot muffler.

His sudden screams of pain filled the night. Carter held him against the muffler with the weight of his body until he was sure the man was mad with pain.

Then he released him and waited.

When Duval struggled to his feet, still screaming, Carter brought his right hand up to the man's mangled throat. He found the Adam's apple with his fingers, and applied all his strength.

Carter felt the throat give inward, and when the screams of pain ebbed to a hoarse death rattle, he dropped him.

He took a full five minutes to get his breath and check his own injuries. Then he dragged the body into the trees.

The motorcycle, on its wheels again, was drivable. He put it on the kickstand and used the headlight to find his Luger.

One last check for debris and he was riding south toward Helsinki.

—From THE ANDROPOV FILE
A New Nick Carter Spy Thriller
From Jove in January 1988